BEST WISHES FROM THE FULL MOON COFFEE SHOP

MAI MOCHIZUKI
TRANSLATED BY JORDAN TAYLOR

brazen
First edition

First published in Great Britain in 2025 by Brazen, an imprint of
Octopus Publishing Group Ltd
Carmelite House
50 Victoria Embankment
London EC4Y 0DZ
www.octopusbooks.co.uk

An Hachette UK Company
www.hachette.co.uk

The authorised representative in the EEA is Hachette Ireland,
8 Castlecourt Centre, Dublin 15, D15 XTP3, Ireland (email: info@hbgi.ie)

Original Japanese edition published by Bungeishunju Ltd in 2021, under the title *Mangetsu Kohiten no Hoshiyomi, Honto no Negaigoto*. English translation rights reserved by Octopus Publishing Group Ltd, under the license granted by MOCHIZUKI Mai (text) and SAKURADA Chihiro (illustrations), arranged with Bungeishunju Ltd through Emily Books Agency Ltd, Taiwan, and Casanovas & Lynch Literary Agency, Spain.

Hardback ISBN: 978-1-91424-099-7
Trade paperback ISBN: 978-1-91424-097-3
eISBN: 978-1-84091-837-3

A CIP catalogue record for this book is available from the British Library

Typeset in 11/18pt Swift LT Std by Six Red Marbles UK, Thetford, Norfolk

Printed and bound in Great Britain

1 3 5 7 9 10 8 6 4 2

This FSC® label means that materials used for the product have been responsibly sourced.

FSC
www.fsc.org
MIX
Paper | Supporting responsible forestry
FSC® C104740

We all looked at the master with moonlight-filled eyes. But I didn't entirely understand what he had just told us. I said, 'Wait, are you sure? Doesn't everyone already know that?'

A black cat – Luna – was suddenly by my side. She murmured, 'When it comes to *that*, a lot of people do seem to know, but they hide it deep within.'

'Huh,' I said, letting out a breath.

This is what the master had said: 'A fun way to know yourself is to know your true wish.'

Contents

The Full Moon Coffee Shop has no fixed location.
It might appear in the middle of a familiar shopping arcade, by the station at the end of the railway line, or on a quiet riverbank.
At the Full Moon Coffee Shop, we don't take your order; instead we bring you desserts, meals and drinks – selected just for you.

The feline messengers of the stars meet below the Moon to study the movements of the celestial bodies.
Soon, they will apply their learnings at the café to help those lost souls seeking solace at the Full Moon Coffee Shop.

I wonder where the master – that large tortoiseshell cat – is tonight . . .

Introduction

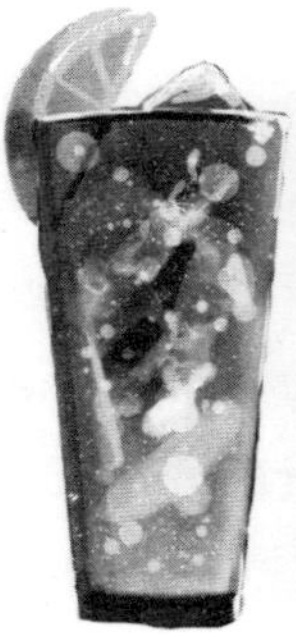

月光のレモネード

A clear, bright half-moon hung in the night sky, and nights like this, with a young moon glowing in the sky, are for study.

The power of the half-moon as it moves towards a Full Moon pours into everything and is helpful for all manner of improvement. That is why our Full Moon Coffee Shop was holding a study session that night. The café's food truck sat beneath the moonlight in the large clearing of a park illuminated by gentle lamplight. Tables were arranged in a fan shape around the truck, while all our companions gathered around the large tortoiseshell cat: the master.

He was both the person in charge of the café and a reader of the stars.

The sky was dyed a deep navy as the sun had now completely disappeared below the horizon, and an early winter wind blew through the park. Yet the area around the food truck was pleasantly bright and warm, meaning we had no trouble studying.

Everyone there that night was what is called 'a connected one'. They are the servants of the stars, but know very little about anything other than themselves, which is why they sometimes came to the master as his students.

Each student was given their own table with a glass of Moonlight Lemonade. It was made from lemons soaked in moonlight, giving the drink a sweetly sour taste that flowed through the body and soul. This drink was recommended for people returning home after a long day at work to help sweep their fatigue away, but it also energised students just starting a study session.

'This lemonade is the exact same colour as my hair,' I chuckled and stroked my hair as I took a sip of the lemonade, then turned towards the master and raised my hand. 'Master, I have another question.'

'What is it, Venus?'

'The age changed from the Age of Pisces to the Age of

Aquarius in the year 2000, but things are only suddenly becoming unstable now, in 2020. Why is that?'

The master nodded in understanding and looked around at the other students. 'Can anyone answer V's question?'

In response, a young man with red hair put his hands on the table and pushed himself to his feet. 'The Age of Pisces ended in the year 2000, and gave way to the Age of Aquarius. But the reason the feel of Pisces has stuck around is that it was still an era of element Earth. That's now ended too – just recently, in 2020. Well, more accurately, in December 2020 – and now we're in Air. So we're now seeing the full effects of Aquarius.'

With that, he sat back down.

He's Mars. He has strong masculine features and glossy red hair, with eyes of the same colour.

'I'm surprised how much M seems to be studying . . .' muttered a silver-haired boy. That's Mercury. He's famous for his androgynous good looks.

'Could you actually call me by my name?' said Mars, with a hard look. 'You're "M" too, you know.'

Mercury smiled and said, 'I guess so.'

The master watched their exchange with a gentle smile, then chuckled and got the conversation back on track. 'Mars, you're absolutely correct. The world was in element Earth for over two hundred years, including throughout the nineteenth century.'

I frowned. I was getting even more confused. 'So, the Age of Pisces started after the previous age and continued for basically two thousand years until the year 2000, right?' I asked. 'But what are these eras of Earth and Air?'

As I spoke, I was getting more confused than ever.

Mercury – who was sitting beside me – gaped and said, 'What? You don't even know that? But you always look so smug when you're giving customers advice.'

'I pretty much get horoscopes,' I said. 'I understand the characteristics of the houses and the planets and that sort of thing. But, it's sort of like I'm just passing on this great revelation I've been given. Like I'm just a conduit, you know?'

'So, you're just going with your gut?'

'It's not just gut! I'm expressing the will of the Universe,' I retorted firmly, but hesitantly at the same time, feeling uncomfortable.

Mercury sighed with exasperated acceptance. He's always such a snarky boy.

Mars glared at Mercury because of what he said. 'V's the planet of intuition. You need to respect her more.'

Mercury responded with a noncommittal sound of acknowledgement.

The master guided us back on track and picked up a pocket watch. Normally it was just an average pocket watch, but sometimes it could do something special.

The images of Pisces and Aquarius appeared in the night sky.

'Like Mars said,' continued the master, 'it was the Age of Pisces for approximately two thousand years up until the year 2000. It is now the Age of Aquarius. When we say it is now the age of a particular constellation, we're really talking about the Spring Equinox. The Spring Equinox was in Pisces, but it has now shifted to Aquarius.'

'The Spring Equinox . . .?' I responded, participating in the conversation even though I still didn't understand.

'As the seasons change, people change what they do and wear, yes?' said the master. 'You could even say they are changing how they live. In the same way, as the ages change, so do various other things.'

I resisted the urge to ask further questions and instead listened to his explanation. Here is what he said: the four elements – Fire, Earth, Air, Water – have been rotating in and out throughout the Age of Pisces. Fire is the beginning. It is associated with the signs of Aries, Leo and Sagittarius. Earth is the build-up, associated with Taurus, Virgo and Capricorn. Air is the turning point, associated with Gemini, Libra and Aquarius.

Water is the conclusion, associated with Cancer, Scorpio and Pisces. The change from one element to another is called the Great Mutation and it occurs about once every two hundred years.

'And these mutations happen . . .' said the master as he strode over to a middle-aged man in a smart suit – Saturn – and a kind-looking middle-aged woman – Jupiter – and put his paws on their shoulders. 'Because of these two. Saturn and Jupiter are planets with a very powerful influence on society. Approximately every twenty years, they align in what is called the Great Conjunction.'

'Conjunction' is an astrological term meaning 'coming together'.

I nodded and wrote 'Great Conjunction' in my notebook. 'Which means Saturn and Jupiter are all nice and cosy with each other once every twenty years.'

Saturn grimaced. 'I'm not entirely sure about that phrasing . . .'

Jupiter laughed beside him and said she thought it was fine, while the master nodded in agreement with me.

'Saturn and Jupiter overlap once every twenty years,' he said. 'And where they are when they overlap changes once every two hundred years or so. For example, changing from an area of the Fire element to an area of the Earth element. They have been meeting in Earth areas – Taurus, Virgo, Capricorn – since around the nineteenth century until the year 2020.'

He paused a moment to tap his pocket watch's crown twice.

'However,' he continued, 'they overlapped in Aquarius, an Air element, in early December 2020. From that point onwards, they will meet at the constellations of Gemini, Libra and Aquarius – all associated with Air – for around the next two hundred years.'

As he spoke, the pocket watch lit up and two diagrams appeared in the night sky.

Finally understanding, I stood up and said, 'All right, I get it now. Basically, it's like this, um, if you don't mind me using my favourite example of the stage as a metaphor.'

I gathered my thoughts before starting.

I began here: as the tale of Pisces unfolds on the stage, the spotlights that are Fire, Earth, Air and Water shift depending on what is happening in the performance. It's the same stage, but a change in the lighting can transform the atmosphere.

The story of Pisces came to an end under the same lighting setup Earth had had for the past two hundred years, ever since the turn of the nineteenth century. Pisces' performance is now done, and Aquarius's

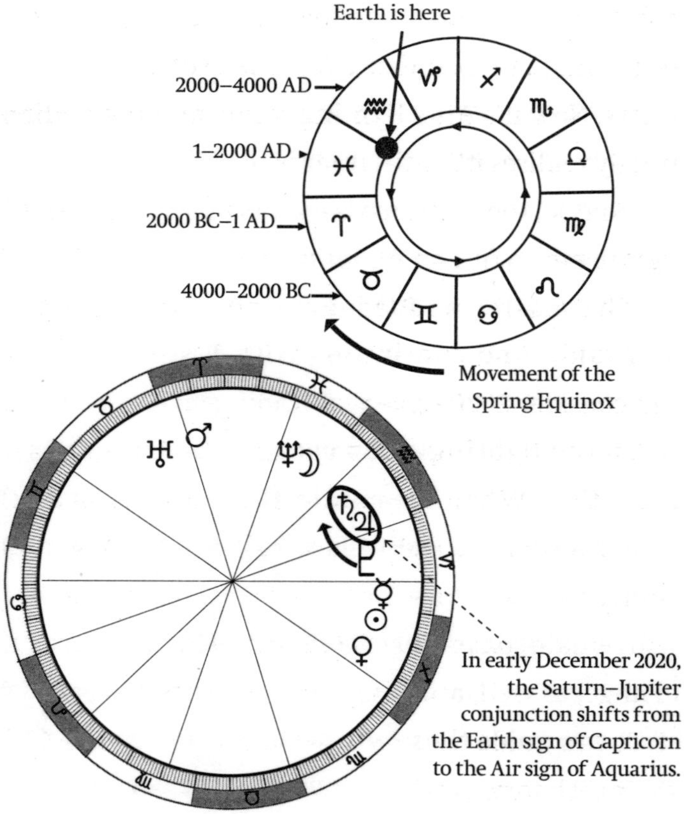

Note: The Spring Equinox moved from Pisces into Aquarius while the planets moved from Capricorn into Aquarius. They move in opposite directions.

has begun, but Earth is still providing the lighting. This means the audience has a hard time noticing the performance is a whole new show, because the atmosphere up on stage feels the same. But, at the beginning of December 2020, the spotlight suddenly shifts. Now it's Air's lighting setup, and the audience finally realises it's a different play.

'And so, the performance waits until it's under Air's lighting to go full-on Aquarius, right?' I said.

The master nodded, amused at my take on it, and said, 'And continuing with V's metaphor, we can consider 2020 – the year leading up to the moment when the lighting setup changed to Air – a year of transition. When the nature of the age changes, the construction of society changes. That's why so many things that defy logic have happened lately. The world will remain somewhat chaotic for several years after the change, as well, and I hope that we messengers of the stars can guide those who have become lost, lighting their path forwards.'

I nodded quietly along with the master.

'Right,' he said. 'It's nearly December – a special season for all sorts of people. I was thinking we might open the Full Moon Coffee Shop again for special holiday hours on Christmas Eve.'

Our faces immediately brightened at that. Normally,

we only opened on nights when there was a full moon or a new moon, but we often opened on Christmas Eve too, even if the moon wasn't quite right.

'And the banquet afterwards too?' I said.

'Yes, the end-of-year party!' added Jupiter, and we broke into laughter.

Mercury shrugged slightly and said, 'What are you ladies on about? Banquet? End-of-year party? Call it what it is: a Christmas party.'

Saturn was the only one among us to remain as calm as always. His expression indicated that he had no interest in partying, but he cared so much about proper decorum that he never failed to attend.

The master watched us, his eyes narrowed in amusement. 'One more thing: I believe this year we'll be able to fulfil those two requests – the one from *him*, and the one from *her*.'

My eyebrows knitted together as I wondered what he meant by that. Luna, though, seemed to know. She gasped and said, 'By *her*, you mean the little one from twenty-one years ago, don't you?'

'What?' I asked. 'What happened twenty-one years ago?'

'My friend. She had one request before she made her journey. I suppose it nearly is time.'

The master nodded. 'And *he* is the one who made

a request fourteen years ago. Oddly enough, both are multiples of seven.'

Uranus grinned and rested his cheek against his fist. 'But Master, seven and its multiples are numbers deeply connected to the Universe. It isn't that odd, is it?'

'You have a seven-year cycle, after all,' said Mercury, and Uranus nodded. 'And old man Saturn drops a trial on people every seven years.'

'Old man . . .?' Saturn objected huffily. 'And it's not a trial. It's a challenge.'

'But, for some people, a challenge is a trial,' I said, but the master told us all to calm down as we were starting to get worked up.

'Let's get back on track,' he said. 'I'll explain those requests later. But considering them, I believe we may have to be open more nights than usual this December, more than just the extra night on Christmas Eve. I'd appreciate help from all of you.'

Everyone chorused a yes in response.

'I don't really get what's going on, but I know I'll have to work hard,' I said, clenching my fists. Mercury gave me a cool glance.

'Working hard is all well and good, but are you sure you can handle this, V?' he said.

'What do you mean?'

'You didn't even know the most basic of astrology basics. Have you been slacking on your studies?'

I winced in response. He'd hit a sore spot. 'Come on. It's like what Mars said before – I'm more of an intuitive type. Besides, I've always been better at tarot cards than at studying the stars . . .'

Jupiter giggled beside me as I made my excuses. She has long, wavy, chestnut-coloured hair and kind of gives jazz-singer vibes.

'Mars did mention it before,' she said, 'but V's job is using fun and intuition. She's not like you, Mercury. She doesn't have your love for studying.'

'Oh, Jupiter!' I cried as I stood and flung myself into her arms.

'That's what's good about you, V,' she said.

'Thank you, Jupiter. You're right. I love fun! That's why I'm hoping the next time we set up shop, it'll be somewhere even sparklier!'

'That does sound fun. And winter is in full swing, which makes me want to go somewhere with lots of pretty Christmas lights.'

Saturn sighed and looked at us with exasperation. He adjusted his glasses, appearing just as grumpy as always. 'Jupiter, must you always be so easy on V?'

'Well, we're friends,' she said.

'Right?' I said, chiming in with her.

Saturn and Mercury looked at each other with resigned shrugs. Mars, on the other hand, added a quiet, 'I don't see what's wrong with them being friendly.'

He may be a young man, but there are some things about him that make him seem more like a boy going through puberty. His tone was blunt, but he was always there to support me.

I raised my head, wanting to show him the best of me. 'By the way, Master,' I said, 'how should people live their lives in this never-ending Age of Aquarius?'

'Hmm,' the master said as he thought. 'The most important thing is for them to know themselves.'

There was a chorus of agreement from everyone, and Mercury said, 'Life is easier when they study their natal chart so they understand the attributes they have as a person.'

'I know that, of course,' I said. 'But is there an easier way to explain it? I sometimes set up on street corners and give out advice, as a sort of apprentice astrologist, and people often tell me they don't really understand what I mean when I start talking about natal charts and attributes.'

Saturn quickly jumped into say, 'Then they should know their challenge.'

'By "challenge", you mean "trial", right? I don't like that. It's not fun,' I said, looking away in disgust.

'Not fun . . .?' His eyes grew wide. He appeared lost for words.

Everyone chuckled at us.

The beautiful woman with perfectly straight black hair – Luna – giggled too and said, 'Perhaps the first thing you need to know in order to know yourself is the Moon's position.' She spoke in a very quiet voice, like she was whispering. Her voice, staggering when singing opera, was otherwise quiet like this.

'The Moon's position . . .' I said. 'That reminds me, for Miss Serikawa, the Moon was in her fourth house, the Home.' As I took notes, I remembered the woman who had visited before.

Luna nodded. 'The houses are important, of course, but also the constellation.'

'You mean the Moon sign?' I added a note about Moon signs also being important.

'And a fun way to know yourself . . .' said the master, as the moon's light seemed to grow stronger.

It had reached its zenith, transforming us into cats. Luna was a black cat, Mercury a Siamese, Mars an Abyssinian, Jupiter a Maine coon, Saturn a black-and-white tuxedo cat, Uranus a Singapura and me a white Persian cat.

We all looked at the master with moonlight-filled eyes. But I didn't entirely understand what he had just told us. I looked at him with my brows furrowed and said, 'Wait, are you sure? Doesn't everyone already know that?'

A black cat – Luna – was suddenly by my side. She quietly murmured, 'When it comes to *that*, a lot of people do seem to know, but they hide it deep within themselves, to the point that they don't really understand it.'

I blinked in surprise, and Luna nodded.

Jupiter smiled and added, 'Like the cave the sun goddess Amaterasu hid in.'

'Huh,' I said, letting out a breath.

This is what the master had said:

'A fun way to know yourself is to know your true wish.'

Prologue

It was a surprisingly warm day in autumn. All sorts of people had gathered in the Science Expo Memorial Park in the city of Tsukuba for the Year End Harvest Festival. There were rows of stalls selling every famous regional food, from Hitachi wagyu beef steaks to lotus-root chips to *hoshi-imo* dried sweet potato, while a troupe of foreign musicians provided cheery music.

They were a quartet composed of a blonde woman and a silver-haired boy playing violin, a red-headed youth on viola and a woman with perfectly straight black hair strumming a cello. Tsukuba was famous for its businesses, including those involved in education and administration research, meaning there were quite a few non-Japanese researchers there. So none of the festival-goers found the quartet of foreign performers odd.

This particular group, though, was very odd. They were as beautiful and brilliant as Hollywood stars, entrancing onlookers.

The only Japanese person in the group seemed to be the conductor. He was a middle-aged man with black hair wearing a suit and a somewhat irate expression shown by the furrow between his brows as he waved his baton.

'That conductor looks intense,' I said, then let slip, 'Maybe he's angry . . .'

Next to me, my seven-year-old daughter Ayu shook her head. 'He looks angry, but he's actually really happy. He's having lots of fun.'

Her voice carried well, and the man seemed to hear. He gave an awkward smile, and the musicians' shoulders shook with laughter while they continued playing. I bowed my head several times in apology, then tried to make our escape. As we left, the conductor turned to Ayu and waved goodbye with his empty hand. He smiled shyly, which made me feel like he'd shown me something incredibly rare and precious about him, and that made me happy.

'He seems nice,' my daughter said.

I nodded.

Ayu was like that. The other day, for example, we had seen an elderly man on the bench in the park next to our house. He came occasionally. He always looked grumpy and only scowled in response when mothers with children like me greeted him.

I didn't like him one bit.

He reminded me of my estranged father. My father was always taciturn and unsociable, but, when he did open his mouth, it was to have his way like some dictator. It was his fault our family fell to pieces. And I imagined this old man was the same sort of person. Why did he come to that park if he hated seeing children?

At some point, I stopped saying hello to him and only gave a curt nod as we passed. Ayu, though, turned to face him and gave him a lively 'Hello!'

He didn't say anything. He just scowled.

One shouldn't respond to a child's greeting like that. I was angry and quietly told Ayu not to worry about it, but she just looked at me in surprise.

'Don't worry about what?'

'The fact that he didn't say hello back,' I said, feeling uncomfortable putting it into words, but Ayu shook her head vigorously.

'You just can't hear him because he talks really quietly. He said hello.'

'You could hear him?'

'No. He mumbled it. I think he's just shy.'

I couldn't imagine that being the case. But when we were on our way home, the man came over to us and held out a sweet without saying anything. Actually, not without saying anything. He did in fact mumble something.

Ayu looked at me to check it was all right for her to accept the sweet, and I nodded.

She took it and said, 'Thank you.'

The corners of the old man's mouth turned up when he saw Ayu's huge grin. Seeing that, I decided that perhaps Ayu was right, that he really was just shy and socially awkward.

Perhaps my father was that sort of person, too.

But then I brushed that thought aside with a chuckle as I stroked Ayu's hair.

There was something mysterious about Ayu. She could sense how a person really was, even when others couldn't tell at first glance.

'Hey, Daddy!' called Ayu, pulling me out of my reverie as I looked at her.

There was my husband, a short distance away from the bustle of the crowd. He gave us a big wave with a huge grin on his face. 'Junko!' he called out to me.

At one point, he'd been the sort of cheerful young man you might see in a painting. Now he was a cheerful middle-aged man.

'Turns out Satomi isn't going to make it today. She's too busy with work,' he said.

Satomi was his younger sister, making her my sister-in-law. We might not be related by blood, but I didn't see my own family much and had always wanted a little sister, so I loved her as if she were my real sister.

'Oh, that's a shame, as she's the one who organised the event!' I said.

'I think, to her, it's just one of all the many events she's involved in,' said my husband. Satomi was an event planner with an advertising firm. She'd left Ibaraki Prefecture for her busy job at the office in Shibuya.

'Oh, Auntie Sato isn't coming?' said Ayu with a disappointed pout. She really admired her aunt. 'That's sad.'

'Ayu, you see that over there? Aunt Sato worked hard on that,' said my husband, pointing towards a row of cages in the plaza.

'Puppies!' Ayu's eyes lit up.

I shaded my eyes with my hand. 'Oh, you're right. There are a lot of dogs and cats over there.'

The animals seemed uneasy in the cages. I looked at the setup, wondering what it was for, and it made sense when I saw the sign: ADOPT A PET – ADD A FURRY FRIEND TO YOUR FAMILY!

'They're running an adoption event,' said my husband with a nod. 'Satomi said she wants to reduce the number of animals in shelters being put down as much as possible, but she isn't in a position to adopt. She decided she could at least help introduce these animals to potential owners.'

By the cages stood an employee in an animal mascot costume and a kind-looking woman. She was talking to the animals, telling them it was all right.

'Mum, Mum, can we go and look?' said Ayu as she tugged at my hand.

I frowned. 'We can look, Ayu, but we can't adopt one. It's a big responsibility taking care of another living creature.'

It was important to help these stray cats and dogs, but we couldn't take one in if we couldn't handle it.

Out of nowhere, a memory flitted into my mind. I was in primary school, back in my family home in Kamakura. I was running alongside the tracks of the Enoshima Electric Railway all the way home. When I got there, I called loudly to my mother, 'My friend's dog just had puppies! They're looking for homes for them. Please, Mum, I want one.'

Then my little brother, who'd arrived home before me, jumped up from where he'd been lying on the tatami-mat floor and said, 'Me too! I want a dog.'

The two of us joined forces, constantly pestering Mum about wanting a dog. We told her we'd take it for walks twice a day, feed it and everything. We'd even finish our homework early and help out around the house. We'd be the best children ever.

Of course we could never live up to those promises.

We whined, cried and threw tantrums until we somehow won our parents over and succeeded in getting a dog. She was a mixed breed that looked a bit like a Shiba Inu and had round eyes that melted your heart. She was well behaved and gentle, and my brother and I fell utterly in love with her. And yet, the walking and feeding and homework and helping around the house only lasted a short while. My mother had to take care of the dog after that, while my brother and I just smothered her with love.

'You two are all talk and no follow through!' my father would say angrily. He'd been against us getting a dog. Whenever he got angry, we'd help look after the dog more – but it never lasted long.

My beloved dog died the first winter after I graduated from university. I'd been so keen to leave home that I went to live in the dorms during university, then, once I found a job after graduation, I got my own place in Tokyo.

I'll never forget the shock I felt when my mother called to say my dog wasn't well. It was a given to me that she would always be there, at home. She was a member of the family. I used to cry every time I remembered.

I swore then that I would never own another dog, or any animal for that matter.

'We can go and look,' I said to Ayu. 'But we're just looking.'

'I know, I know,' she said as she moved towards the cages.

The lady working there saw Ayu and her eyes turned into smiling curves. 'Well, hello. Master, we have the cutest customer.'

She was a plump, middle-aged woman, and not Japanese. Her long, wavy, chestnut-coloured hair was gathered in a ponytail. She wore a frilly apron over her beige dress, which made her look as if she was about to bake a pie or some cookies.

The person she called 'Master' – the one in the mascot suit – turned to face us. He was wearing a tortoiseshell cat costume and I presumed, based on its size, that the person inside was a man. The costume was so convincing that I couldn't help letting out a gasp at how incredible modern technology was.

The tortoiseshell master sported a tie and a white shirt with a dark apron on top. His bespectacled eyes crinkled in a smile when he saw us.

'Hello! Welcome!' he said.

'Hello!' said Ayu, vigorously. Then she immediately turned to look at the cages. The animals that had all looked frightened a moment before were now looking at her with shining eyes.

'They're all happy I'm here,' said Ayu. She looked at each one, then crouched down in front of what looked like a fully grown mixed-breed dog. The dog stared at Ayu with its round eyes. 'I want this doggy to come home with us.'

'I've always dreamed of having a dog, too. Ever since I was little,' said my husband.

'Not you, too,' I said, putting a hand on my forehead.

'If this doggy comes home with us, then I don't need any birthday presents or Christmas presents,' said Ayu.

'Such a good girl, Ayu,' said my husband.

'You be quiet,' I said, and he clamped his mouth shut. 'Why that dog, Ayu?'

There were smaller and cuter cats and dogs there. That one actually seemed the mangiest of them all.

'Because this one is really lonely,' said Ayu.

'Oh, Ayu . . .' I shook my head in frustration. 'Owning a pet is a big deal. You're responsible for their life.'

'That's kind of amazing, isn't it? It's like you're doing God's work,' she said, with a carefree smile.

'And you say amazing things, Ayu,' said my husband. He was impressed, but I was lost for words. She was probably just another young child saying things without truly knowing the consequences. But she had struck a chord in my heart. God's work?

Without replying to her, I crouched down to look at the dog in the cage.

'She's already big, but she's a sweetheart. Would you like to try holding her?' said the master, taking the dog out of the cage and gently cradling her in his arms without waiting for our response. His hands moved with such dexterity and care that it was hard to believe he was wearing a costume.

He held the dog out towards me. I was a little taken aback, but I took her in my arms. I felt her soft fur, her warmth, her beating heart.

This was the feeling. In that moment, I was taken back to when my dog was alive. I was the one who insisted we get a dog, but then my mother ended up taking on all the responsibility while I did nothing.

My eyes grew hot with tears, and I squeezed the dog in my arms. 'You're right. Being responsible for another life is like doing God's work,' I murmured in a choked voice.

Ayu smiled and agreed. I looked down at the dog and smiled in resignation. Ayu would probably only take care of the dog in the beginning, like me, when I was a child, then I'd be responsible after that.

But maybe that was fate.

My husband put his hand on my shoulder. I nodded. I had no choice. Then I looked at the master and said, 'We'd like to adopt this dog. Is that all right?'

I had had a feeling this would happen when Ayu said she wanted to go and see the animals, tugging at my hand.

I watched Ayu squeal with joy and throw her hands in the air, the dog wagging her tail as if she understood. I shrugged, wondering if this really was for the best.

'Thank you,' said the master. 'This little one is happy to make such a wonderful connection. If you don't mind, I'd like to move you over here to go over the details. Would you like a drink?'

I looked towards the back of the plaza and saw a food truck with a Full Moon mark on it. Maybe it was their logo. There was a sign in front of the truck that said Full Moon Coffee Shop.

'A pop-up café?' I asked, and the master nodded.

'We have some coffee ready for you,' he said.

When he said that, the eyes of the plump woman beside him shone. 'It's not often you serve coffee to someone this young.'

I winced at that. I was far from young.

'It's a thank-you for creating this bond today,' said the master. 'As well as a sort of encouraging cheer to say, "Good luck!" '

He must be talking about the start of our new life with the dog, right?

'I also think we may be meeting again soon,' he continued. 'And I hope I can serve what I have prepared for you then.'

'Meet again soon?' I asked, but quickly realised he must be referring to when we come to pick up the dog. 'Of course. I look forward to seeing you again, too.'

I bowed, genuinely excited for it.

'If you don't mind joining us over here, then,' said the master. 'I also have a café au lait for your husband and a hot cocoa for the little lady.'

My husband grinned happily. 'You know, lately, my stomach's been a bit uneasy, so I tend to enjoy café au lait more than normal coffee.'

'And I love hot cocoa!' Ayu piped up.

The three of us joined hands and went over to the Full Moon Coffee Shop.

Chapter 1

Cancer's Cheese Fondue and Sagittarius's Candy Apples

Satomi Ichihara

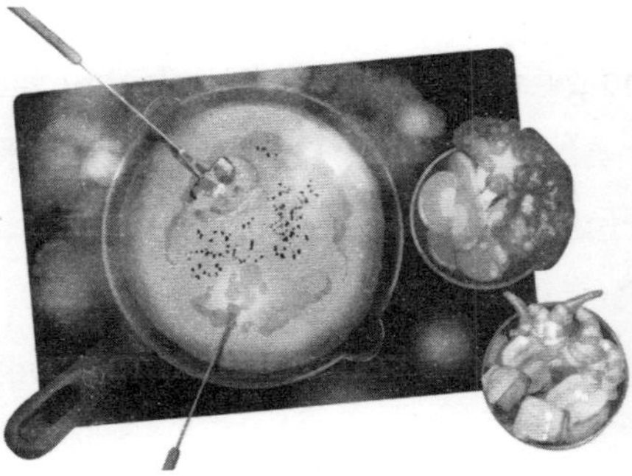

蟹座のチーズフォンデュ

射手座のりんご飴

1

'Oh, jeez . . .'

I was sitting in the corner of our bustling office with my phone in my hand, sighing. I checked my calendar and realised we were already in December. I swear autumn had only just begun.

'At this rate, Christmas is going to be here in a flash,' I grumbled, complaining about what I should do. The girl sitting at the desk next to mine craned her neck towards me.

'What's wrong? Did you get another annoying project?' she asked, looking concerned.

Her name was Koyuki Suzumiya. She was a young temp brought onto my team to help out during this fiscal year. I was impressed by how she was always looking out for the people around her.

'Thanks for asking, Koyuki, but it's not work. It's personal,' I said.

She grinned, seeming relieved. 'It is almost Christmas. I bet you're getting buried in date invites, aren't you?'

I couldn't help smiling at that. 'Oh my gosh, Koyuki, no. Well, you're right that it's an invitation for a Christmas date, but it's from my boyfriend.'

My eyes dropped to my phone which now sat on my desk. My boyfriend's message was still on the screen:

> Satomi, I really want to spend Christmas Eve with you this year. Do you think you can make time? I don't care how late you get off work, I'll wait.

Satomi was, of course, me. And it seemed Koyuki had seen the message, too. 'It's always busy on Christmas Eve in this line of work. I know he wants to see you, but some things are just impossible . . .'

I sighed and agreed. For someone in charge of events for an advertising agency, Christmas Eve was just another workday, not a day to spend with my boyfriend as it was for everyone else in Japan. He was well aware of that, too.

'He did say he doesn't care how late you get off work, though. Maybe you can manage something?' said Koyuki.

'Yeah, that is true, of course . . .'

I felt an unwavering determination in his message.

We'd started dating nearly seven years ago, during university. But in all that time, he'd never said anything like 'Satomi, I really want to spend Christmas Eve with you this year' or 'I don't care how late you get off work, I'll wait.'

He was going to propose.

My head dropped into my hands. Koyuki looked at me with confusion as I told her my suspicion.

'Why is that a problem? Most people would be happy their long-term boyfriend was going to propose on Christmas Eve.'

'I don't want to get married yet. I'm too comfortable with my current lifestyle.'

I turned around and stared out the window. Our office was connected to Shibuya Station, and my flat was in Ebisu, about twenty minutes' walk away. I had a convenient, picture-perfect life in which I could even cycle to work on sunny days.

'Your boyfriend,' said Koyuki. 'Didn't you meet when you were both at the University of Tsukuba?'

'Yeah. He's a lecturer there now.'

'That's amazing,' she said, clutching her hands together in excitement.

'But that's the problem . . .'

Tsukuba, in Ibaraki Prefecture, was my hometown. I had studied at the university there. When people talked about that university, it was always about how there were a lot of couples who lived together as students or got married after graduation. Some even went so far as to say, 'The countryside is boring and there is nothing to do, so people just get married.' But it's surprisingly untrue. Ibaraki always ranks low on lists of the most desirable prefectures, but it's actually a nice place to live.

My brother's wife comes from Kamakura and even she says that the city is ideal for her life. And out of all the towns in Ibaraki, Tsukuba is one of the most academic. It has lots of research facilities run by large companies. The city itself is very pretty, with spacious parks as well as fancy international cafés and shops. In terms of the right environment for raising children, nothing beats Tsukuba. That's why so many people decided they liked it enough to settle down there.

But I was still in love with Tokyo. Tsukuba just lacked something for me. My boyfriend wasn't going to quit his job at the university, either. That meant that if I wanted to keep working at my job, I'd have to commute to Shibuya from Tsukuba. Though my company had a branch office in Tsukuba and they'd most likely let me transfer there if I requested it. It was difficult to transfer from a branch to the main office, but easy to go the other way.

My parents would be happy, too, because I'd be closer to them. But I'd worked so hard for the life I had now. Maybe it was an old-fashioned value from the time of the bubble economy in the TV programmes I watched, but I'd always admired the woman working hard in Tokyo. It wasn't something I wanted to let go of.

'Well, you don't have to think about transferring right away,' said Koyuki. 'What if you commute for a little while to start with and think about it later? Doesn't Tsukuba have the Press train or whatever?'

'Express. It's the Tsukuba Express.'

'Yeah, that. I'm pretty sure it only takes forty-five minutes to get from Tsukuba to Akihabara on that.'

'Still . . .' I said with a half-smile.

'Besides,' continued Koyuki, 'you could always consider living separately.'

I shook my head. 'If we're going to be living separately, I don't see the point in forcing the relationship to be something other than what it is now.'

'I guess not,' she said. 'Is your boyfriend originally from Tsukuba?'

'His family is from Tokyo, but he hated how jumbled and confused Tokyo feels. He went out of his way to choose Tsukuba. He's the polar opposite of me.'

He was always saying, 'I like cities like this, with lots of green,' but I'd always assumed he'd find a job in Tokyo after graduation. I never expected him to stay at the university . . . But that was just the sort of person he was. Laid back, kind, warm. I could see how the atmosphere of Tokyo just didn't suit him.

And I honestly did love him. I treasured the time I spent with him. I didn't want to marry him, but I also definitely didn't want to break up with him. If I turned down his proposal, though, we might very well end up separating.

And that was why I said, 'This is a mess . . .'

I was potentially standing at a fork in the road, one where I had to choose between love and career.

My phone suddenly vibrated on the desk, causing me to jump. It was probably him. Afraid, I checked the screen to find the caller was Junko Ichihara.

My sister-in-law.

'She doesn't often call me . . .' I murmured. The two of us were as close as real sisters and we texted regularly, but she rarely rang me.

I wonder why she's calling?

I picked up my phone and stood up from my desk to go out in the hallway. 'Hi Junko. How are things?'

'Satomi, that event you planned was so much fun.

Thank you for putting it together.' That was the first thing she said.

'Oh, you mean the event at the Science Expo Commemorative Park. I heard you adopted a dog.'

'Yeah. But there's a bit of a long process, so she hasn't come home with us yet. We'll be able to bring her home on Christmas Eve. Ayu's so happy.'

'You didn't go out of your way to adopt her just because it was an event I put together, did you?' I asked, feeling apologetic, but Junko cheerily said no.

'I think it was fate. I needed to thank you.'

'Oh, no. You don't have to thank me. So, what made you call?'

'Right, so, after the adoption event, we stopped by Iias, and there . . .'

Iias was a large shopping centre in Tsukuba. It was as big as a town in and of itself, with so many different shops it was hard to imagine there might be anything you couldn't buy there. During my days at uni I used to go regularly. Actually, it was still somewhere I had to go every time I went home to visit the family.

'. . . I saw Ryo at the jewellery store staring at the rings, and I called out to him before I could stop myself. He gave some excuse about looking for a Christmas present for you.'

Ryo was my boyfriend. My shoulders heaved with a sigh of frustration as I listened to Junko babble excitedly. If he were planning some wonderful surprise, then word like this from a relative would ruin it. Junko was normally so thoughtful. It didn't seem like her to spoil a surprise . . .

'I wasn't really sure if I should tell you,' she said, 'but you're always saying how you're not ready to get married just yet, so I decided I should give you a heads-up.'

I was lost for words. To be perfectly honest, no matter how often I'd imagined it happening, if I were to be suddenly presented with an engagement ring, I might say something like, 'I'm . . . I'm sorry.' And that would create a rift between the two of us.

Junko was warning me because she was worried about how Ryo and I were at different places in terms of our desire for marriage. She may not be my sister by blood, but she was always looking out for me and, for that, I was grateful.

'Right . . . Well, thank you,' I said.

'That's okay. Oh, one other thing.'

'What is it?'

'Do you remember when you were here not that long ago and told Ayu you'd show her around Tokyo?'

My mouth hung open at the sudden change in topic, but I nodded and said, 'Yeah, I remember saying that.'

'Not that long ago' was actually in summer during the Obon holiday season, though. My precocious niece, just old enough to be in her first year of primary school, kept excitedly asking me, 'Auntie Sato, Tokyo is really fancy, isn't it? Is it amazing?'

Junko had pouted in annoyance and said, 'Hey, I've taken you to Tokyo before.'

'But you only took me to Ueno Zoo and stuff,' replied Ayu, mirroring her pout.

I laughed at the pair of them and said, fine, I'd be happy to show Ayu around Tokyo. I promised her she could come and stay with me any time she wanted.

'Well,' said Junko on the phone, 'ever since you said that, Ayu's been asking when she can visit you. The onslaught is never ending. But recently, she's started talking about how she won't be able to go to see you anymore because the new dog is coming. It sounds like she's given up . . .'

Junko seemed to feel bad bringing it up, but I shrugged off her discomfort. I might have talked about Ayu visiting without thinking much of it, but my niece had taken it seriously as an event to look forward to. Four months had passed since I'd promised her that she could come, and she had probably been waiting this entire time for me to suggest a date. If that were truly the case, then I'd done something quite awful. Junko likely hadn't mentioned it before now because she knew how busy I was.

'Junko, I'm so sorry. You don't have the dog yet, right? Then, how about this Saturday? I just happen to have the day off.'

This time of year would be good, too, since the city was aglow with Christmas lights.

'Are you sure?' said Junko, sounding a little surprised.

I chuckled and nodded. 'I'm sure. She probably won't be able to make it out for her birthday, after all. So it'll be a sort of early birthday present from me.'

'Thank you, Satomi. All right, I'll bring her to Tokyo.'

'I appreciate it. If you don't mind taking her on the Express to Akihabara, I'll pick her up there.'

'Thank you so much. She'll be so happy. We've got her new clothes especially for the occasion.'

There was a pang in my heart at that. She even got new clothes just for this? Ayu had been looking forward to visiting me so much, and I'd completely blanked.

Oh, Ayu, I'm so sorry.

'All right, well, see you Saturday, then. Just let me know what time you'll be in.'

'I will. Thank you again.'

Having ended the phone call, I returned to my desk.

'Was that your boyfriend?' asked Koyuki, burning with curiosity.

I grinned and said, 'Nope. I have a date with someone else now.'

She blinked several times in shock.

'And she's the cutest girl ever.' I quickly showed Koyuki a photo of my niece I had saved on my phone. 'Here's my date.'

Koyuki burst into laughter and said, 'Oh my gosh, isn't she adorable!'

'That she is.'

'Is she family?'

'My brother's daughter.'

'Your niece? I have a brother who's quite a bit younger than me. Oh, little kids are just the cutest thing in the world.'

'Yep. I love her like a granddaughter.'

'Granddaughter? Well, I guess that's not too far off. You can spoil her without having any of the responsibility.'

We laughed in agreement.

'Right, well, I need to get to work so I can focus all my attention on my date with this little cutie,' I said, getting into the right headspace as I turned back to my monitor.

2

The promised Saturday rolled around. I was waiting at the ticket gates of Akihabara Station as agreed when Junko and Ayu appeared. Ayu wore a red duffel coat and shiny shoes. Her hair was usually straight, but today it was done up in curls. She looked like a doll. I smiled when I saw her.

'Thanks again, Satomi,' Junko said apologetically, her hands pressed together.

I shook my head. 'I've been looking forward to this, too.'

'Okay. Let's meet back here tomorrow. Call me right away if anything happens. Oh, and just in case.' Junko handed me a 10,000-yen bill and Ayu's health insurance card.

'I'll take the card, but you don't have to give me money,' I said with a smile, refusing the cash. 'All right, Ayu. Shall we go?' I took her little hand in mine.

'Ayu, make sure you listen to your Aunt Sato,' said Junko.

'I will,' piped Ayu.

'I hope you enjoy your time in Tokyo, too, Junko,' I said.

Ayu and I gave Junko a big goodbye wave and left.

'Ayu,' I said, 'where do you want to go first?'

I looked down at her, and she looked up at me with sparkling eyes. 'Tokyo Skytree!'

'Skytree?' Earlier, I'd researched all the shops and cafés that a little girl might enjoy, so I found myself wondering why she'd choose such a corny place.

'Me and Yuka are the only two out of our whole class who haven't been to Tokyo Skytree. And Mum just keeps saying, "We'll go soon," ' said Ayu huffily.

'Oh,' I said, my shoulders shaking as I tried to keep myself from laughing. I was pretty sure Junko didn't find the Skytree exciting enough to bother trekking all the way to Tokyo for.

I wonder if she's enjoying her day out in Tokyo without having to look after a child.

'All right then, let's go to Tokyo Skytree,' I said.

'Yay!'

We set off at a brisk pace.

'Now, how should we get there?' I said.

It was easy enough going by train, but maybe the bus would be better, because then Ayu could see the city she'd come all this way for.

With that thought, I decided we'd walk a short distance to a bus stop to get on a Toei Bus to the Skytree. I imagined Ayu would enjoy seeing Asakusa through the windows.

As the bus set off, Ayu pressed her face against the glass. 'Wow.'

She looked up, her eyes widening.

Everyone who comes to Tokyo from the countryside is always looking up. Once you get used to living in the city, you stop doing it. Whenever I used to visit, I'd always find myself staring up at the high-rise buildings, feeling the power of the city, my heart gripped with intense longing. But now, days went by without me ever turning my eyes upwards. I realised then I never really took in the sights around me. My eyes were always cast down as I walked . . .

I was hit with a vaguely painful feeling and the corners of my mouth tugged up in a self-denigrating smile.

Tokyo Skytree came into view as the bus crossed the Sumida River. Ayu clapped her hands together and her eyes shone as she cried loudly, 'Wow! It's so big. Wow!'

I realised it was also my first time seeing the Skytree from this close. 'Yeah, it's amazing.'

I heard chuckles around us while Ayu expressed her awe with her entire body. Anyone looking at us would probably assume we were a mother and daughter visiting from the countryside. If I were Ayu's mother, I might feel embarrassed that we were making such a scene, but being her aunt, I was just filled with warmth like the people watching us.

'All right, Ayu, stand there.'

'Okey dokey!'

We arrived at the Skytree, and I captured the moment with my phone. We moved to go inside, but Ayu grimaced at the long queue spilling out the door.

'Do you want to wait in the queue to go in? Or do you want to go somewhere else?' I asked.

'I just wanted to see the Skytree from up close. Let's go somewhere else.'

'You sure?'

'Yeah. My friends said there's nothing special about the inside anyway.'

She was right. On the outside it was a very tall

building, but inside it was just your average shopping centre.

'Where should we go next, then?'

'I want to go to Harajuku!' Her voice rang out, seemingly instantly, like she'd prepared her answer. Tokyo Skytree and Harajuku? Both unbearably cheesy places. But today I was happy to accompany her anywhere.

'All right. Next stop: Harajuku!'

3

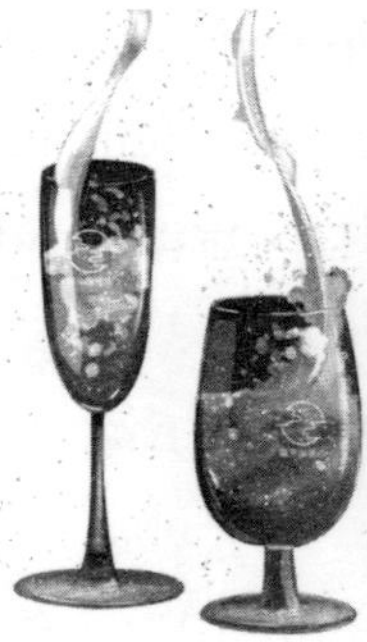

星屑のワインと昼と夜のミックスジュース

'Wow, it's like a festival!' said Ayu excitedly the moment she glimpsed Takeshita Street after we got off the train at Harajuku Station.

Every part of Tokyo was filled with people, but Harajuku in particular evoked a feeling of celebration. The hip stores lining either side of the narrow street probably made Ayu think of the path leading up to a shrine during a festival. I bet that was exactly what she was after.

'That's cute. Oh, that's cute!' she said, her eyes sparkling as we walked.

Her eyes landed on some crepes, and she spun around

to look at me, her skirt twirling as she did. 'Auntie Sato, can we have one? I brought my allowance.'

'Sure, but it's my treat.' I bought a crepe, and we shared it beneath the winter sky.

After that, we spent quite a while in a Kiddy Land shop, and before I knew it the sun was hanging low in the sky.

'You must be getting hungry,' I said.

'Nope, I'm not hungry at all.'

She was probably so excited that eating was the last thing on her mind.

'That's right,' I said. 'I planned to take you somewhere special today.'

'Somewhere special?'

'It's near my flat. It's a beautiful, sparkly place.'

Ayu jumped up and down. 'Oooh, I want to go!'

We went back to Harajuku Station and boarded the Yamanote Line towards Ebisu Station. The promenade at Yebisu Garden Place had been garlanded with winter lights. Now was the perfect time to see them, with the sun setting in the background. It was probably going to be hard with the crowd, but we should manage to catch a glimpse.

Ebisu Station was only five minutes away from the promenade. We hopped off the train and heard music that reminded me of the advert for Yebisu beer. It was a surprisingly long walk through the station, but the moving walkway of the Sky Walk meant even young Ayu wasn't worn out by the distance.

Yebisu Garden Place had originally been the site of a Sapporo brewery, but had since been turned into a large complex filled with all sorts of things. Its big winter attraction was the Christmas lights display consisting of around one hundred thousand bulbs and one of the world's largest Baccarat chandeliers. It was also known for the huge Christmas tree in the clock plaza, which was visible as you walked down the street.

'Woah.' Ayu stood in front of the lights, and a tremor ran through her body.

'Amazing, right?'

The crowd alone was a sight to behold, though we weren't quite packed in like sardines, probably because the sun hadn't fully set yet.

Ayu nodded vigorously.

'When I was a kid, I saw a TV programme being filmed over there at the clock plaza and I decided then I wanted to live in this city when I grew up,' I said.

It had all started with simple fascination. At some point, that fascination had turned into a dream, which in turn became a goal. And I had achieved it.

Visiting this place now overwhelmed me with emotions, including a little frustration. I wanted to be involved with an event this large someday. I chuckled at myself. Turned out I was right; I couldn't just quit my job to marry my boyfriend.

'Wow, it's like we're swimming in the Milky Way,' said Ayu.

'Oh, what a lovely thing to say, Ayu.'

We took some photos in front of the Christmas tree in the clock plaza before walking along the sloped promenade to the central square, where we came to a stop. I stretched and said, 'All right, I really am starting to get hungry.'

'Me too.'

'I thought you might be. Where should we eat?'

We had the best chance of finding somewhere if we decided on a place now and made a reservation. Just as I was thinking that, Ayu let out a little gasp of excitement.

'What is it?' I asked.

'I just saw a fluffy white cat telling us to go over there.' Ayu made a 'come here' gesture with her hand.

That's ridiculous, I thought, but when I looked, I too saw the tail of a white Persian cat slipping away between the waves of the crowd. Oddly enough, none of the passers-by seemed to notice it. Ayu and I exchanged a look, and then chased after it. We followed the cat through the crowd and emerged in the plaza in front of Château Restaurant.

The square had been crammed a moment earlier, but the crowd seemed to have receded like a wave pulling away from the shore. A large moon hung in the night sky, whose colours went from crimson red through to navy blue. Beneath the moon stood the castle-like restaurant, with a single food truck café parked out front in the plaza. The sign said FULL MOON COFFEE SHOP.

The white Persian cat we had seen a moment before was on a table in front of the truck, its fluffy tail waving back and forth.

'Oh, there's the kitty,' said Ayu as the cat leaped into the food truck. 'That café was at the place where we got our doggy, too . . .'

'Really?' I said, though Ayu sounded as if she was talking to herself. If they had been at the adoption event, that meant they were at Science Expo Memorial Park. I had been instrumental in planning the event, but I didn't know every single business that was involved.

'Well, a food truck can go anywhere . . .' I said, though, as we approached the café, I did wonder exactly how they had managed to squeeze the vehicle in.

'Welcome,' said a close-to-two-metre-tall tortoise-shell cat as he stepped out of the truck. He was wearing an apron over a white shirt and tie.

I gawked in astonishment, but Ayu just let out a sound of recognition. 'That cat was there, too,' she said.

'At the park?'

'Yeah. He's called "the master".'

'Oh.' I let out a sigh, feeling a little relieved. It was just a pop-up café with a mascot called the master. Even so, I was surprised at how high-quality the cat costume was.

The master invited us to sit down, gesturing with his paw to a table in front of the truck. The promenade was still bustling with people, so I couldn't understand how there was barely anyone here in the Chateau Plaza. I was a bit hesitant, wondering what was going on, but Ayu took a seat and cheerfully said, 'Hello! Can I have something yummy?'

I smiled awkwardly and placed my hand on her back. 'By "something yummy" she means, may we please see the menu?'

But the master shook his head. 'At the Full Moon Coffee Shop, we don't take your order; instead we bring you desserts, meals and drinks – selected just for you.'

Ayu nodded along. 'They said that before, that they don't take your order.'

'Oh, really? Well, I suppose that's sort of fun,' I said with a nod, though I couldn't help thinking it was a bit pushy for a café.

'Normally, our café opens only on the night of a full or new moon. This month, however, is special. We open on any night when the moon is particularly beautiful,' said the master.

This month was probably special because it was Christmastime. Essentially, this café didn't take orders and only opened twice a month. It probably wasn't someone's primary business. More like a fun side hustle. Which meant they were likely passionate about what they did, so I could expect good food.

Ayu and I settled down at our table and signalled that we were ready to be served. The master chuckled and turned to Ayu. 'It's lovely to see you again.'

'You too! And thank you for the dog. I can't wait for her to come home.'

'Please take good care of her. We'll be back shortly to serve you.'

With that, the master returned to the truck.

Ayu and I waited for the delicious food we were about to be treated to, on the edge of our seats in anticipation. After a short time, two beautiful women flowed out of the truck. One was blonde; the other had black hair. Their manes were tied back into ponytails and they wore black aprons over white shirts. They must have been wearing coloured contacts, too, since the blonde woman's eyes were an intense blue and the black-haired woman's were purple.

'Thank you for waiting,' they said as they gracefully

placed plates and cups of water on the table. The plates carried all manner of steamed vegetables: broccoli, carrot, courgette, potato, pumpkin and lotus root. There were also cocktail sausages, thinly sliced bacon, boiled prawns and pieces of French bread. In the centre of the table, the ladies then placed a small gas burner, which they lit before placing a cast-iron pot on top that was filled with soft, molten cheese.

'Cheese fondue!' Ayu and I both cried, our eyes glittering.

'That's right,' said the blonde woman with a smile. 'This is Cancer's Cheese Fondue. The cheese has been imbued with moonlight. Please enjoy it with these vegetables, showered in abundant sunlight.'

The black-haired woman followed that by holding out a bottle of wine. 'Please pair it with this Stardust Wine.'

This woman's expression barely changed as she spoke to us in a flat tone. She seemed very cool and aloof. She didn't wait for me to respond before pouring the wine into a glass. It looked like normal white wine, not the fizzy sort, but I thought I saw tiny twinkling stars swirling through the liquid.

'And for the little lady, we have Day and Night Mixed Juice,' said the blonde woman with a wink as she poured Ayu a glass. This drink was a stunning swirl of pale yellow and violet. Both Ayu and I gasped as we leaned in to stare at it.

'It's so beautiful,' said Ayu. 'Is it grape juice?'

'Yes, but not just grape juice. It also has lemon juice in it.'

Ayu grimaced at the mention of lemon. 'I don't like sour things.'

But the woman just gave a chuckle. 'Don't worry. These lemons have been showered with the dazzling light of the sun, giving them a very delicate sweetness. The grapes were left to bathe beneath the light of the moon, so they have a rich sweetness.'

Which made sense, seeing as it was called 'Day and Night' Mixed Juice.

'Thank you!' Ayu said, her eyes sparkling.

'Please, enjoy your meal.' The two women bowed. The black-haired one walked briskly away, while the blonde gave Ayu a little wave before returning to the truck. They both looked like Hollywood stars.

I watched them go, then Ayu said, 'Cheers, Auntie Sato!' as she picked up her glass. I quickly turned my attention back to her and smiled as I picked up mine. We both had wine glasses, though Ayu's was different. Its stem was short and squat, possibly because it was meant for kids and less likely to break if it was dropped.

'Wow, I'm all grown up,' said Ayu. She seemed over

the moon to be holding a wine glass, too, and seeing that made me happy. We clinked our glasses together, and I took a sip of the nicely chilled Stardust Wine. It had a sharp dryness to it, but also a faint sweetness.

I squeezed my eyes shut. 'This is lovely. I feel it flowing right through me.'

Ayu also took a drink of her beautiful juice. 'It's not sour at all. It's so good!' she said in surprise, a smile spreading on her face.

'Shall we eat, then?' I said.

'Yeah!'

We put our hands together in thanks for the meal, and then picked up our fondue forks. I speared a piece of French bread and dipped it into the pot. The cheese oozed as I lifted my fork back out, almost sparkling. I quickly carried the bread to my mouth. There was none of the sharpness of an aged cheese, but all the rich flavour. And yet, that richness melted away, leaving behind a delicate milkiness in your mouth. It was every bit the sort of taste both children and adults could enjoy.

This is wonderful. What sort of cheese is this anyway? I thought as I took another sip of my wine. That's when I noticed the superb harmony between the cheese and the wine, and my hand flew to my mouth. I was squeezing my eyes shut, barely able to contain my joy, when I heard Ayu say, 'Oh, the master.'

I turned and saw the cat mascot stepping out from the truck with a tray in his hand. He came over and placed a dish of small, round croquettes on the table.

'I'm sorry to keep you waiting,' he said. 'Here is the main course for you: Cancer's Cream Croquettes. Please, try them with the cheese.'

'Cancer's Cream Croquettes? Are they crab and cream croquettes?' I asked.

The master nodded. I smiled and said, 'I was wondering why we were having Cancer's Cheese Fondue when we're in Sagittarius, but it's because the main is these crab croquettes, isn't it?'

The master's eyes crinkled. 'That is part of it. But the other reason I prepared this for you is that your Moon sign is Cancer.'

'Cancer? No, I'm not a Cancer. I'm a Scorpio.'

'No, your Moon sign. May I show you your natal chart, which details your Moon and Sun signs?'

I gave a vague sound of approval, my mouth hanging open. The master took out a pocket watch and pushed the crown down with a click. The clock's face burst into light, projecting a diagram that resembled a map into the night sky.

Ayu gasped, her eyes gleaming. 'Master, you're like a magician.'

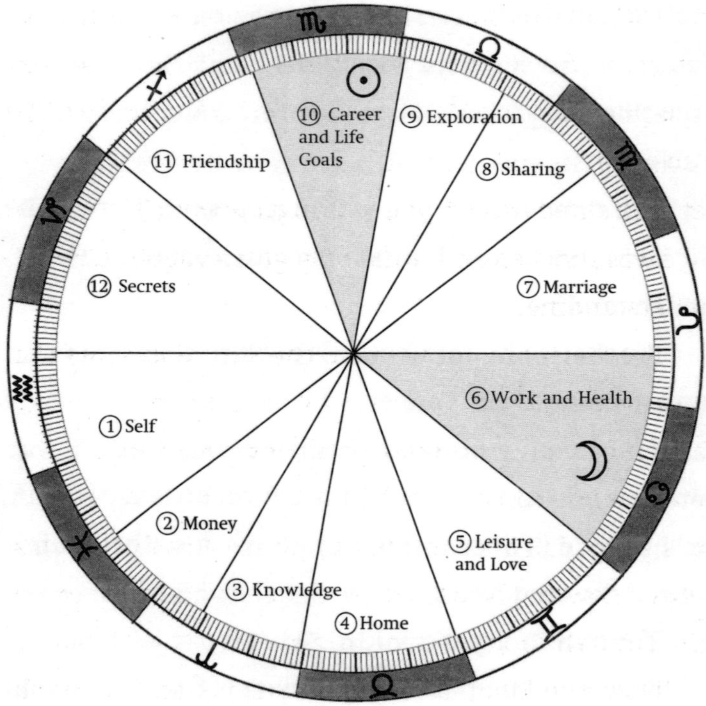

I swallowed the urge to tell her it was just a projection and agreed.

Projected into the sky was a horoscope based on Western astrology. The circle was divided into twelve numbered sections. I looked closely and saw the Moon was located in the section marked six and the Sun in the section marked ten.

'The Sun is in your tenth house,' said the master. 'As you can see, written here on your natal chart, the tenth house is about career and life goals. People who have their Sun in this house show a strong predisposition for business. This suggests you ambitiously pursue success as defined by yourself. Your Sun sign is Scorpio, which also suggests you never falter in your studies, and you set high standards for yourself in your work.'

I was shocked and could only give a vague sound of understanding.

'Furthermore, for women, the Sun represents the masculine. Perhaps you have a strong respect for your father, or you want your partner in marriage to be someone you can respect.'

I gulped. This sounded accurate. My father was retired now, but he used to be a teacher, and I respected him from the bottom of my heart.

'Now, the Moon is in your sixth house. The sixth house rules work. I can tell from your natal chart that you are a workaholic, busy day in and day out with your job, but that you actually feel most comfortable with it that way. With the Sun in your tenth house and the Moon in your sixth, you are clearly about work down to your very core.'

I found myself nodding along in agreement.

'However, your Moon sign is Cancer. So you need one other place where you can feel comfortable.'

Sitting outside the section of the circle occupied by the Moon was the symbol of Cancer: ♋

'Is a Moon sign different from a normal sign?' I asked.

The master nodded. 'What you call a "normal" sign is your Sun sign. Your Sun sign is your exterior, while your Moon sign is your interior: your true nature, your instincts, the most basic part of you. And your Moon is in Cancer. You feel the deepest sense of relaxation when in a Cancerian environment.'

I looked at the master wondering what sort of environment that might be. 'A Cancerian environment?'

'Well . . .' began the master as he started to explain Cancer. Everything he'd said before had seemed to fit me perfectly. It was just this Cancer thing that wasn't really clicking. I let out a sigh of exasperation, but Ayu leaned in towards the master. 'Hey, Mister Cat. I'm a Sagittarius. I was born on the tenth of December. It's nearly my birthday.'

The master smiled and nodded as if he'd known that for a long time. 'And your Moon sign is also Sagittarius, so I've prepared a Sagittarius-themed dessert for you. I think it may help you feel better too, judging by your Cancer Moon,' he said, looking at me. 'I hope this becomes the night you discover your true wishes.'

He bowed and stepped away from the table.

'True wishes . . .?' I said. What did he mean by that?

I sat there with my brows furrowed in thought,

while Ayu leaned forwards with sparkling eyes. 'Auntie Sato, these croquettes are so yummy.'

'Oh, yeah.'

I speared one of the croquettes – as round as a planet – with my fondue fork and dipped it into the cheese. I took a bite and found the pairing of the croquette's creaminess with the cheese enhanced the flavour of both.

We continued eating, raving in between mouthfuls about how good it was. Dessert was served just as we finished the main course.

'These are Sagittarius's Candy Apples, coated with stardust sugar. We make candy apples from apples pierced with Sagittarius's arrows.'

And, just as the name implied, there were arrows speared into the tops of the apples. Their candied shells gleamed in the light, and they were coated in what looked like golden icing sugar. The arrow was actually a knife you could easily pull out and use to cut up the treat. The apple's core had been removed and the space filled with warm honey, which made cutting through the apple much easier than I expected.

When I cut into it, I saw that the flesh of the candied apple was actually in two layers: the section under the skin was cool and crisp, but the inner flesh had been turned into a compote. Both paired perfectly with the crunchy candied exterior. The warm honey in the centre spread outwards to mingle with the apple flesh, creating an experience that melted in my mouth. I found myself tensing my hands in ecstasy.

'This isn't like the candied apples I've had at festivals,' said Ayu as she chomped down on hers. I agreed wholeheartedly.

'This isn't anything like any candied apple I've ever had, either.'

'Does that mean it's not really a candied apple?'

'No, it is. Different places do different things and end up with very different products, but they're still candied apples.'

'That's amazing.'

'Yeah. I've never had a candied apple this luxurious before.'

We polished off every last crumb, even our desserts. After a thoroughly enjoyable time, we stood up to pay, which was when we found that we were no longer in the plaza.

4

'It was like a dream . . .' The vague thought crossed my mind as we left Garden Place. I let out a long, slow breath. It really had been like a dream. The very moment we stood up after we had finished eating, a wave of people had suddenly washed across the plaza. I'd turned to the truck to pay for our meal, but it had already disappeared.

I had no idea what to do. Would this be considered a dine-and-dash situation? It was the restaurant itself that had disappeared, so you couldn't really say we had dined and dashed.

I was weighing our options as Ayu tugged at my hand. 'Auntie Sato, there's a convenience store.'

That snapped me back into the present, and I nodded. We'd talked about stopping by a shop. 'All right. Want to go in and pick up a few things?'

'Yep. I love convenience stores.'

We filed inside and bought bread for the next day, as well as snacks to eat at my place later.

'At home, Mum gets angry if I eat snacks late at night,' said Ayu, looking uneasy as we left the shop. I chuckled, holding a finger in front of my lips. 'This is a special occasion. Just make sure you brush your teeth properly.'

'Okay! This is special,' she said energetically.

My flat was within walking distance of the station. I say flat, but it was really nothing more than a tiny studio.

'Woah, it's so tidy,' Ayu said the moment we stepped inside. She spread her arms as if to gather what she saw up in them. I'd gone to the effort of tidying up before she came, but I was also serious about having a sleek setup because I'd always admired city living.

'You'll sleep up there tonight,' I said, pointing to the lofted sleeping area.

'Really? That's so cool! But what about you?'

'Don't worry. I'll sleep down here. More importantly, Ayu, shall we start our after-party with a toast?'

'Yeah, let's have an after-party shindig.'

She took the snacks out of the shopping bag and lined them up on the table. Ayu had bought grape juice, and I a beer.

'Cheers!'

We clinked our drinks together.

'Ayu, you like grape juice, don't you?'

'The juice at the café was so good I kind of wanted more. But the convenience store didn't have mixed juice.'

'I'm not sure anywhere else sells that sort of drink.'

Ayu nodded, giggling. 'That lady's hair was the colour of lemons.'

'It was. Beautiful golden hair the colour of sunshine. And the black-haired woman's eyes were so beautiful. Like the colour of grapes.'

It was almost as if the juice symbolised the two of them.

'The lady with lemon hair was really cheerful, and the lady with black hair was really shy,' said Ayu.

'You think she was just shy?' I had found her cool and aloof.

'Yeah. She was really shy.'

I remembered Junko saying something about how perceptive Ayu was. If Ayu was right, then the woman's flat tone and emotionless expression weren't because she was blunt, but simply timid.

How cute. I smiled at the thought.

'Are you always sensing things like that, Ayu?'

'Things like what?' Ayu looked at me blankly, apparently not knowing what I was talking about.

'Uh, nothing. Hey, Ayu, tell me everything that's been going on lately. How's primary school? I bet it's different from nursery school.'

'It's so different. I'm a big girl now that I'm in primary school,' she said with an excited huff, puffing up with pride.

'But I remember you crying when nursery school ended because you didn't want to leave.'

'That was forever ago,' Ayu said with a pout. I laughed and agreed it was a long time ago.

'Oh, there was this one time . . .' Ayu said, trying to dive into a story, but she kept rubbing her tired eyes.

'Ayu, why don't you brush your teeth and go to bed?'

'Okay.'

She brushed her teeth, rubbing her eyes as she did so. I wondered if she should take a bath, but decided she was so tired it'd be best to leave it for the morning. I laid her down to sleep in the loft, and then came downstairs. I decided I should at least check my email before going to bed, so I opened my laptop and got to work.

After a while, I heard sobs from upstairs. My eyes

widened, and I hurried back up the ladder. 'Ayu, what's wrong?'

She was pressing her face into the pillow as she sobbed. Shaken, I moved to her side and rubbed her back. 'Ayu, are you in pain? Is everything okay?'

'Mummy . . .' she said in a strangled voice, her face still cast down.

'Oh, Ayu . . .'

She might look like she had things together, but she was still just a little child. She simply wanted her mother once night fell and she started to feel frightened.

'It's okay, Ayu. Your mum's going to come get you tomorrow,' I said, lying down next to her.

'Auntie Sato . . .'

She snuggled her small head against my chest. I stroked her hair, thinking how utterly sweet she was. We'd had such a fun time during her visit, but she still just wanted her mother. I realised I had been the same when I was young. One time I went to stay at a friend's house in the neighbourhood, but once night fell, I started crying. My parents had to come and get me. It wasn't my father I clung to then, in tears; it was my mother.

My mother had been a stay-at-home mum. I was happy to have her always by my side, but she seemed to have no freedom at all. Seeing my mother bending over backwards to please my father was what made me want to be an independent woman. It was around that time that my brother married Junko. They were the same age – twenty-five – and had met at university.

Junko worked, just like my brother. Their relationship was one of equals, and they respected each other. I admired them so much and became so enchanted with them that I wanted the same thing for myself.

They had had a hard time getting pregnant, which was a very painful experience for Junko. She underwent fertility treatments for a long time. But their efforts bore fruit in the end when Junko became pregnant with Ayu. To me, though, the whole thing seemed an ordeal.

After Ayu was born, Junko became a stay-at-home mum. Ayu might be a sweet, well-behaved child now, but she had been a handful when she was an infant because she cried constantly. I had realised then I would never manage that sort of thing myself and, to be entirely honest, I never had understood Junko's decision to sacrifice her entire career to spend time with a child.

Now, though, I felt as if I was beginning to understand it a little more. To Ayu, there was nothing in the world more important than her mother. Perhaps Junko felt that every minute, every second in which she was still Ayu's whole wide world was so precious that she didn't want to miss any of it, so she chose to be with her always. It was so important to Junko that she was willing to sacrifice everything she'd built in her career for it.

I pulled Ayu's small body into an embrace and softly closed my eyes. As I listened to her gentle breathing, I whispered, 'Maybe I'm just the tiniest bit jealous of Junko.'

The moment the words crossed my lips, what the master had said at the Full Moon Coffee Shop flitted through my mind.

5

The next day, Ayu and I went back to Akihabara Station.

'Ayu! Satomi!'

Junko was already in front of the ticket gates. I bet she'd got there far earlier than we'd agreed to meet.

'Mummy!' Ayu flew towards Junko the moment she saw her.

'Did you have a nice time, Ayu?'

'Yeah! We went to Tokyo Skytree, then Harajuku, and then we had cheese fondue in front of a castle at night,' Ayu rattled off like a machine gun.

Junko nodded along and then looked at me. 'Thank you so much, Satomi.'

I shook my head. 'I had fun, too.'

'But even one day can be a struggle. Really, thank you. Anyway, Ayu, say thank you to Auntie Sato,' Junko said as she knelt down to look into Ayu's eyes.

Ayu nodded and turned to me. She gave a deep bow. 'Thank you so much, Auntie Sato!'

I bowed back.

'All right, should we get going?' said Junko.

'Okay. Bye bye, Auntie!' Ayu waved with a big grin on her face as she and Junko walked away.

'Bye bye, Ayu.' I smiled as I waved back, with a cloudy cocktail of mixed emotions filling my heart. There was relief because I'd returned her to her mother safe and sound. Release because I was freed from the responsibility of caring for a small child. But the overpowering emotion was an enormous feeling of loss.

Oh no, I feel like I'm going to cry.

Ayu's pigtails bounced as she walked away, her small figure becoming smaller and smaller. I felt a sharp tingling in my nose as I watched her go. Maybe she felt my gaze on her, because she turned back and gave a huge wave goodbye. I was struck with such loneliness that I found it difficult to breathe, but I waved back just as big.

I cannot cry.

It would be silly for me to cry. My niece came to stay for a night and was now going home. That was all. And yet, the dam broke and tears spilled down my face the moment Ayu and Junko disappeared from view.

I had no idea I could cry so hard, but there I was, hot tears pouring down my face. And that's when it finally struck me.

I hope this becomes the night you discover your true wish.

I remembered the master's explanation of Cancer. Apparently, it represented home and family. I had the Sun in my tenth house and the Moon in my sixth. Working suited me, but at the same time, my Moon sign was Cancer, which meant I longed for home and family. It hadn't seemed to describe me when he first said it, though I'd since realised it might explain why I sometimes got a powerful urge to visit my family back home. But that wasn't really it. That was just a smokescreen.

I had felt, for a long time now, that I was nearing my limit. I loved my job, but I was about to burn out. Whenever I felt it coming, I sought quality time with my kind boyfriend or went back home to visit my family. But every time the word 'marriage' crossed my mind, I quickly swatted it away. Seeing my mother and my sister-in-law, I'd convinced myself that I had to choose between work or family. That having both was a luxury I couldn't afford. And if I had to choose just one, I'd choose work.

I loved my job. I'd built my dream life through hard work. But there remained one wish I couldn't let go of. Deep in my heart, I knew I wanted my own family.

Then I met the master at the Full Moon Coffee Shop and finally realised what I'd failed to notice deep inside myself. Before I knew it, the dream had turned into a nightmare. I kept telling myself, as if under a spell, that I wanted this life, that I admired this life, that I was happy in it.

Maybe that special night I spent with Ayu had freed me.

'I can't believe I didn't even know how I really felt . . .' I was murmuring, wiping away my tears, when my phone pinged.

It was a message from my boyfriend.

> Any news about Christmas Eve? I don't mind, no matter how late you'll be.

My hand flew to my mouth. I'd never replied to him. My lips turned up into a smile as I tapped a reply out to him.

> I'm sorry I didn't reply sooner. I'd love to spend Christmas Eve with you. I'll finish work as early as I can.

I also wanted to spend that special day with him. He replied with a sticker that said 'Thanks!'

Oh, jeez. I feel like I'm going to cry again.

I still loved my job and I still loved Tokyo. That hadn't changed. It wasn't like I'd decided I would give up everything for him. But I knew we needed to talk about the future. I had no idea what would happen, but I wasn't going to run away. I would face it head on.

I needed both work and family. It might be a luxury, just like that candied apple was, but I still needed it. That was just the star I was born under. Anyway, for the time being . . .

'I'll work hard so we can have a wonderful Christmas Eve.'

I wiped my tears away and walked off, feeling purified.

Chapter 2

New Moon Mont Blanc and a Night of Miracles

Koyuki Suzumiya

新月のモンブラン

1

My dad died in a traffic accident around Christmas when I was eight.

My stepdad appeared around Christmas when I was sixteen, and my baby brother was born around Christmas when I was eighteen. Something about being home made me uncomfortable, so when I started college I left to live on my own. Before I knew it, I was twenty-two, a full-blown member of society.

As for Christmas, I hate it.

'Don't worry about it. I'll go to the shopping arcade for you.'

I was giving Satomi Ichihara, my boss at this temp

job, a full-faced grin. She frowned apologetically. 'Are you sure?'

'I'm sure. You finish early. You'd promised your boyfriend you'd see him tonight, right?' Her expression didn't change. I gave her my firmest look. 'Work is important, of course, but I think your personal life matters just as much.'

'You say that, Koyuki, but you're working on Christmas Eve. Isn't it a special day for you, too?'

'Of course! But I don't have plans until late at night.'

'Do you have a late-night date with your boyfriend?'

'No, I don't have a boyfriend.'

'What are your plans then?'

'One of my favourite pop idols is doing a livestream Christmas performance at midnight. I've been looking forward to it for *so* long. I've got loads of time to kill before then, and a temp like me is always grateful for overtime.'

I clenched my fist and spoke animatedly until she gave a relieved smile. 'All right, if you insist,' she said. 'You really don't mind taking over today?'

'Not at all!' I said, holding my head high.

'I can't believe I'm going home at a normal time on Christmas Eve. I think this might be the first time I've done that since I started this job.' Satomi pressed a hand to her chest in disbelief.

I gave a slight smile of agreement. 'Christmas Eve is a busy day for event planners like you, after all.'

I said it like I wasn't one of them, because I wasn't. I was an outsider.

I'd finished secondary school with utterly average grades, and decided going to a business college and gaining some skills was better than going to some mediocre university. But after finishing college I struggled to find a proper job. I ended up as a temp, hoping to work my way into a permanent position.

It had been two years now.

I've always been pretty capable. I had some specialist skills, which meant I never struggled to find a temporary placement, but I'd already passed through several companies and none of them had offered me a permanent position. Lately, I'd been feeling as if getting one was nothing more than a pipe dream.

Right now, I'd been sent to work for the event planning department of an ad agency. When I heard I'd be working in event planning, I imagined the sort of glamorous job you see on TV, but this department didn't handle anything that large-scale. I'd mostly been working on a lot of small events for neighbourhood associations or smaller cities, towns and villages. A town official would contact us with a plan for an event in their community, then ask us to advise on how to handle everything. I'd started by creating flyers for these events and had graduated to handling advertising work.

I used to meet our clients face-to-face when I first started, but recently, I'd largely been doing deskwork. Even so, I'd still often make an appearance at the actual events to say hello. It might seem a little old-fashioned in the age of the internet, but meeting someone in person and talking to them could have a big impact. And it could be the thing that led to the next thing. Well, at least that's what our team leader, Satomi, always says.

'I really do feel bad, though, Koyuki. And you only just went to the event in Ibaraki for me . . .'

Our team had helped with a Year End Harvest Festival in Tsukuba, Ibaraki Prefecture, not that long ago. Satomi had planned to go there herself to do the greeting, but something came up that she had to deal with and I was free, so I went instead.

'Oh, don't worry about that,' I said. 'I helped set up that event.'

She smiled. 'That's true. And you're the one who proposed the adoption event.'

'Yep. So, how about you let this temp make some nice memories while she's here, since she was involved with the project to begin with?'

Satomi was lost for words. My contract was due to end in March.

'Right,' I said. 'I'll head off to the venue.' With a teasing smile, I picked up my tote bag.

'Thank you, Koyuki.'

'No worries. Just leave everything to me.' I gave her a salute and left the office.

When I stepped out into the hallway, I heard someone say behind me, 'Koyuki's always so cheerful and lively.'

'Yeah. Even though she's a temp, she's always the one to brighten the team's mood.'

Most people would be happy to hear that. But as I stepped into the elevator alone, my expression went blank. They always said the same thing, no matter where I went: 'Koyuki's cheerful, she's lively, she jokes around and creates a fun atmosphere in the office.' It was true. I knew it was, because that was the facade I put up. That was the character I performed.

I looked out over Shibuya through the glass walls of the elevator. The city was alight with colour. It was December, after all. The lights would only shine brighter when night fell. At first glance, it looked beautiful, dazzling even, but if you inspected it more closely, you could see the grime.

The elevator pinged and the door opened. I put

a smile on my face and stepped out into the ground-floor lobby. Our office had excellent access to transport links, with a direct connection to Shibuya Station. I hopped on the Yamanote Line, running clockwise via Shinjuku, and let out a sigh.

2

It was about thirty minutes on the train. I was heading to Yanaka Ginza, the shopping arcade near Nippori Station. The district's official mascot – a cute cat character – was everywhere as I walked down the main street. The large trees were decorated and there were lots of children who looked as if they were having fun.

'Thank you so much for coming out. It's because of you we were able to host such a wonderful occasion,' said the person from the association who had proposed this event. He was a not-quite-yet-elderly man wearing a Santa hat and a smile as he bowed to me.

'It was nothing,' I said. 'I'm just happy it turned out so well.' I bobbed my head in a series of bows, and then looked back towards the main street. There was a banner hanging across the road that said CHRISTMAS ON THE STREET. Crowds of smiling locals wearing Santa hats had gathered under it. There were a lot of children, most of whom, for whatever reason, were unable to spend Christmas with their parents. The goal was to help them have fun, even if only a little bit, so the shopping arcade had requested support from the local primary school to put on this Christmas event.

'The children's happy faces speak to how incredible this event truly is,' said the old man with a shy smile. 'This shopping arcade didn't originally rely on tourists, but high streets are struggling all across Japan these days.'

I nodded, a pained expression on my face. It wasn't uncommon to see shuttered windows along shopping streets. It felt as if lively, crowded ones were becoming more and more of a rarity in recent times.

'The locals are our priority, not the visitors,' continued the man. 'I believe we as a shopping arcade must have local roots in that we support the locals and the locals support us, so that the locals like us. I appreciate tourists, of course, but I'd rather build the sort of place a local will want to visit three times a week than somewhere a visitor might come once a month.'

I nodded again.

'Oh, that reminds me. Before you arrived, I received an email from Ms Ichihara,' he said.

'Oh, she feels terrible she couldn't make it today,' I said quickly in apology, but he just smiled kindly.

'Her email said the idea to do an event for children who can't be with their parents for Christmas came from none other than you.'

I scrunched up my shoulders. 'I wouldn't really call it a proposal . . .'

It was more that Satomi had run with the jumbled mess of words that flopped out of my mouth and turned it into something.

'Really, though, I'm so glad we went with it,' he said. 'There are far more children who can't be with their parents on Christmas Eve than we imagined. Either both parents work, or it's a single-parent home, or what have you . . . Every child is facing their own situation. But children are our region's treasure. I want them to grow up locally, where possible, but it's not really that simple. At the very least, we can make this a special day to remember.'

The event included a Child Dinner Ticket which allowed the children to eat whatever they wanted in the shopping arcade. There were games and stalls like at a festival, as well as a movie screening later. Those silly little words I'd uttered had turned into an event filled with children's laughter thanks to the knowledge and support of lots of people.

'Thank you, Ms Suzumiya,' said the man as he bowed to me, and my eyes started to sting. I bowed my head low too, to hide my tears.

'No, thank *you*. I know I can't do much, but please put me to work somewhere,' I said, flexing my bicep to show that I was strong enough to be useful. We did this all the time: show up at the event we'd helped plan and then stay until the end helping out in some other way. They didn't ask us to, and we weren't forced to, but I'd learned from watching the others on the team that this was best. But the man shook his head and refused.

'I appreciate the offer, but we have plenty of help.'

'Oh, but . . .'

'Today is a special day. You should spend it with those important to you,' he said with a smile.

I couldn't argue with him, so I just gave a meaningless smile back.

'Oh, and,' he continued, 'if you like, you can take one of our strawberry Christmas cakes.'

I shook my head apologetically. 'Thank you, but I live alone. I couldn't possibly eat the whole thing.'

'Oh.' He gave a slight shrug and seemed to find that unfortunate. To be honest, it probably would have looked better if I'd just accepted the offer. I usually would have gone on about how happy I was and accepted the cake, even though I was well aware I couldn't eat it all. But his saying he thought I should spend the day with people who were important to me had triggered a different response.

I plastered a smile on my face in an attempt to change the mood. 'Well, again, thank you so much. I think I'll have to stop by the shops here in my free time at some point.'

'Please do. We look forward to your visit.'

I bowed one last time and walked away. I smiled when I came across the cat mascot walking down the street. I left the shopping arcade and walked the short distance to the station. I was nearing it when I noticed a sign at the bottom of some stone steps that said SUNSET STAIRS.

'Oh, these are the famous Sunset Stairs?' I murmured. I hadn't realised on my way to the event. I started walking up them, but halfway up I stopped and turned around when I felt warmth on my back.

The sun was just setting, dyeing the stone steps orange with its light. At the bottom of the steps I could see the beginning of the shopping arcade. The faint sound of children's laughter reached my ears. It was a level of beauty the city lights could never reach. The sight felt like something straight out of the Shōwa period, but still alive, breathing and spreading warmth.

I felt as if I were witnessing a miracle. And I felt tears threatening to come again, so I gently pressed my fingers to my eyes.

Just then, my phone vibrated in my coat pocket. I checked it and saw a message from my mum.

> Happy Christmas Eve, Koyuki! Thank you for the present you sent Sei. I know you said you're busy today, but will you manage to make it home tomorrow for Christmas? Sei keeps saying how much he wants to see his big sister.

She also sent a picture of my little brother – not even five years old yet. He had on a Santa hat and was holding the toy train I'd bought him, smiling a smile that said he didn't have a care in the world.

Both of us were born in December, me on the 18th and him on the 23rd. That's why my name is Koyuki – meaning 'small snow' – and his is Sei – meaning 'holy'. It was nice because it meant I could get Sei one present for both his birthday and Christmas.

I moved over to the side of the stairs to quickly tap out a reply.

> Ah! I'm so glad he liked it! He is just too adorable in that Santa hat! I wish I could make it for Christmas but I'm running around like a headless chicken at work, so I'm not sure I can. I hope you have a nice Christmas though!

My response was just as lively and cheerful as always, the perfect picture of the 'older sister who loves her little half-brother'. I added a 'Happy Christmas!' and pressed send. Then I let out a sigh and continued climbing the stairs.

I could hear Christmas music. Couples and families were walking down the street, looking happy. Loneliness struck me, like a chilly wind blowing through my heart. I bit my lip and felt a slight pain as my teeth touched the chapped, dry skin.

I clucked my tongue in annoyance.

What is this all of a sudden?

I'd thought I'd left my loneliness behind a long time ago. I must just be sensitive to this bitter wind after experiencing the kindness of the shopping arcade. And the friends I usually relied on to fill the hole in my heart were spending the day with their boyfriends or families. I didn't have a boyfriend, or a family home to go back to. Well, I did, but it was home for my mum, my new dad and their son. It wasn't my home. And I'd never managed to find a permanent job. I was like a migratory bird. I reached the top of the stairs and sighed again.

'Here. We're holding a Christmas event,' I heard someone say at that same moment. It was a friendly voice. I turned around, assuming it was about the event at the shopping arcade, and was surprised to see two glamorous boys. They weren't Japanese, but they spoke fluently as they handed out flyers. One of them had flamboyant hair that was blond on the outside, with a pink layer underneath. The younger, androgynous-looking one had silver hair and a blank expression.

They were both beautiful. And yet the people walking by didn't seem to notice them.

Maybe they're scouts for a modelling agency?

I gave them a surreptitious look, thinking the whole thing was a bit odd. Out of all the people passing by, only one besuited man in his late thirties took a flyer.

'Would you like to experience art on Christmas Eve?' I heard one of the boys say, and I finally understood. They had to be advertising an art exhibition. That would explain why people were ignoring them and trying to avoid making eye contact, since most didn't want the hassle of dealing with someone trying to sell them expensive art. I nodded in understanding, and all of a sudden, the blond boy's face was right in front of mine. My eyes widened.

'Hello there,' he said. 'Please, here you go.' He grinned, showing his teeth as he handed me a flyer. It said: 'Asakura Museum of Sculpture – now with Christmas lights display!'

'The Asakura Museum of Sculpture . . .' I murmured. If I remembered correctly, it was an art museum run by the Taito City government.

'It's just a short walk from here. Please, feel free to visit,' said the flamboyant boy as he pointed to the simple map drawn on the flyer. This was a proper art museum, so there was nothing fishy about any of it. I didn't really feel like going home straightaway anyway. Maybe this was just the thing I needed. My eyes fell to the flyer, and my feet just started walking of their own accord.

Just as the boy had said, the Asakura Museum of Sculpture was only a few minutes' walk from the Sunset Stairs. On display were pieces by a sculptor called Fumio Asakura who had been active from the Meiji to the Shōwa period, in the first half of the twentieth century. The exterior of the museum was predominantly black and the building had a curved entrance, giving its fusion of Japanese and Western architectural styles a retro yet fresh feel. The trees in the garden were alight with decorations. They did have a Christmas light display on after all.

The museum normally closed at half-past four, but it had extended opening hours today. And yet, there were only a very few people there.

To be honest, there weren't enough Christmas lights to impress. I imagined most of the people who visited the museum weren't even aware of the display. Which explained why the boys were passing out flyers: they didn't want the special effort to go unnoticed.

Just as I was putting the pieces together, a man in his late thirties passed me and entered the building. It was the man in the suit who had taken a flyer from the boys earlier. I squinted at him, feeling like I'd seen him somewhere before.

Where did we meet?

No matter how hard I racked my brains, though, I couldn't remember. I let out a sigh and said, 'Oh well.'

As I moved towards the museum, I saw a parked food truck, though the museum grounds were hardly large. It had a sign out front with a full moon on it. It appeared to be a pop-up café. It had a cute vibe, but there was no one inside. I guessed they served drinks during the day.

I wondered about it as I entered the building.

3

ブラックホールのチョコ仕立て

It wasn’t often an art museum asked you to remove your shoes when entering, but this one did. I placed my shoes in a plastic bag, paid the entrance fee and picked up my ticket and a guide booklet.

Before continuing down the hallway, I opened the booklet and read about Fumio Asakura. He came from Oita Prefecture, on the island of Kyushu, graduated from the Tokyo Fine Arts School (now the Tokyo University of the Arts) in 1907 and went on to become a leader of Japanese sculpture and the first sculptor to be awarded the Order of Culture.

I let out an impressed sound before following the path through the museum into the first gallery. My feet came to a stop in front of a large sculpture of a moustachioed gentleman in a suit sitting in a chair. President Abraham Lincoln instantly popped into my head, though the model for this statue was Jutaro Komura, a diplomat of the Meiji period. My breath also caught in my throat when I saw the standing statue of Shigenobu Okuma, prime minister of Japan during the First World War. I wasn't well versed in art, but Fumio Asakura seemed to be the sort of artist who could instil his sculptures with the gravitas of his models. I continued along the path, feeling as if I was meeting the auras of the greats of the period.

The building itself had once been Asakura's home and studio. I passed through his study into a hallway with hardwood floors leading to a door of latticed wood and glass. Through the windows was a courtyard with a perfectly manicured Japanese garden. Everything up to that point was in an old-fashioned Western style from the Shōwa period, but then the building suddenly transformed into a Japanese manor house. I went up to the first floor and looked down into the courtyard. Large, multi-coloured koi swam in the pond.

'I feel like I'm in a high-class ryokan,' I said. Both the building and the scenery were amazing. 'I never realised there could be anything this incredible in a residential area.'

I looked around, impressed. I then put on my shoes to go out onto the roof and stepped out onto the external stairs. Before going up, I noticed another display below, so I decided to ignore the recommended path through the museum and check that out first.

It was the Orchid Room, which had once been a conservatory. The roof was constructed in a triangle made of glass with a large circular window in the middle of the wall. The walls and ceiling were painted pure white, which made me think they should rename it the White Room.

'Or, really, the Cat Room,' I said when I realised that all the sculptures in here were of cats. Sleeping cats, hunting cats. I could almost hear their slow, sleepy breathing, almost feel them about to pounce.

Fumio Asakura must have really loved cats.

'How cute . . .' My heart filled with warmth, and I was glad I'd come.

Finally, I decided to go up to the rooftop garden. Apparently, it was one of the first rooftop gardens in Japan. I came to a halt the moment I stepped outside, and my eyes grew wide.

The sun had set, and the sky was dark. The rooftop plants twinkled with decorative lights. What surprised me most was that I saw a sign for the Full Moon Coffee Shop. Added to it were the words 'Special Christmas Eve

Hours'. The garden was not all that large, but there was a small bar that could seat two.

'Welcome,' said a member of staff wearing a cat mascot costume with an apron, while gorgeous foreign members of staff smiled at me. There was a woman with black hair and another who was blonde. The young man with pink and blond hair who had been passing out flyers was also there, along with the silver-haired boy.

'Oh, you came. That's awesome!' said the pink-and-blond-haired boy with his teeth-baring smile as he came over and put an arm around my shoulder. The black-haired woman muttered quietly, 'Uranus, that's sexual harassment.' He jerked away and apologised.

'Please, have a seat at the bar,' he said, this time indicating the counter in a gentlemanly fashion. I thanked him with a small smile and sat in one of the seats at the bar. It was such a magnificent setup that I could hardly believe it was a pop-up venue.

There was another customer there. It was the man in the suit I'd seen twice already. He'd been sitting at the counter when I arrived.

I . . . definitely feel like I've seen him somewhere before.

He was quite handsome, so I doubted I would have forgotten him if we had met. I snatched a sidelong glance at him. Our eyes met, and I immediately looked away.

'Hello,' he said, and I smiled awkwardly back at him. 'It's been a while.'

I took in a sharp breath.

'You don't remember me, do you?'

I looked at him in puzzlement and gulped. He did look familiar. I'd definitely seen his face somewhere before. Maybe I'd worked with him at one of my temp jobs?

What do I do? I can't remember at all.

Since I didn't know who he was, I had no idea how to act. My eyes darted around in panic.

'I guess I really put you on the spot, asking you that,' he said. 'Sorry.'

He sounded apologetic, but his smile remained carefree. He didn't seem like a bad guy at all.

'Um . . . So, have we met before?' I asked timidly.

His eyes widened, and then he gave a short burst of laughter. 'I guess you really don't remember me. That's sad.'

I apologised and shrunk back.

'It's all right. It is what it is. Anyway, do you live around here now?' he said, smoothly changing the subject.

I shook my head. He really did seem to have known me a long time ago. 'I was just on my way home from work,' I said.

'Meaning, you're going home to a Christmas party?'

'No. I don't live with my family, and I don't have a boyfriend. So, no party.'

The moment I spoke I realised it might come across as if I was emphasising my loneliness to try to hook up with him. I didn't want him getting the wrong idea, but just as the thought crossed my mind, his expression suddenly turned serious and he murmured, 'Oh, I see . . .'

What was that about? I thought, looking at him in confusion.

'Well, how about we have our own little Christmas party then?' he said, and I blinked in surprise. But before I could even begin to feel confused, he turned to the member of staff in the mascot costume and lifted a hand. 'All right, Master, could I get something for the two of us?'

The cat, this 'master', bowed and left the rooftop.

'Um. Did you just order "something"?' I asked.

'Oh, the Full Moon Coffee Shop doesn't take orders.'

'What?'

'What the master serves is exactly what the customer needs.'

'But what if he serves something you don't like, or something you're allergic to? What then?' I said, seriously.

The man nodded and laughed. 'If that were to happen, you could just say, "I'd rather not have this," couldn't you?'

'I don't know if I could.'

'Really?'

'Really. I'm always observing others, figuring out how to pretend to be a good person . . .' I laughed at myself. I couldn't believe I was saying this to a stranger, even if it was a stranger I recognised from somewhere. But there were some topics that were off limits with people you interacted with regularly.

I looked away from him just as one of the servers bounced towards us. She was a young woman with blonde hair and blue eyes, as beautiful as a Hollywood actor, and emanating an air of innocence. 'Let me welcome you again to the Full Moon Coffee Shop,' she said. 'My name is Venus, but everyone calls me V. I just want to let you know that the food and drinks will take a little longer than usual as the kitchen here is downstairs.'

She placed two glasses of water in front of us. I suddenly remembered the food truck parked just outside the museum. 'The kitchen, that's the food truck downstairs, isn't it?' I asked.

'Yep.' She nodded and then held up a finger. 'Do you mind if we chat until it's ready? There's something I'd really love to ask you.'

'Me?'

'Yep. Do you know what your true wish is?'

I was taken aback by the question. 'My . . . true wish?'

She nodded emphatically. 'The master was telling me not too long ago that it's important for people in this era to know what their true wish is. But I thought, do people really need to figure out what it is they truly wish for? Doesn't everyone already know?'

I made some vague comments as she continued in perfect Japanese.

'And then, Luna – the girl over there with black hair – said a lot of people do know, but they hide it so deep within themselves that they can't remember what it is. What do you think?'

I folded my arms across my chest in response.

Now that I really think about it, what is *my true wish?*

I said the first thing that came to mind: 'I'm pretty sure mine is to win the lottery.' The man beside me gave a short burst of laughter, and Venus frowned slightly, as if she had doubts about what I had said.

'Why do you want to win the lottery?' she asked.

'What? Well, because you can do whatever you want if you have money,' I said.

'And if you had enough money to do whatever you wanted, what would you do?'

'Um, I'd travel and go on a shopping spree, buy a flat, quit my job,' I said, then made a show of laughing.

Venus's expression was serious as she peered into my face. 'Are those things your true wish?' Her blue eyes had flecks of gold in them and were as beautiful as a cat's. The force of her stare made me look away. 'Those wishes are superficial. They're not what you truly want. It looks like the master and Luna were right . . .' she murmured. Then, with an apologetic look, she said, 'I'm sorry, but I don't think that wish will come true.'

I grimaced and shrank back. 'Well, yeah. I know. There's no way I'm going to win the lottery.'

She shook her head. 'That's not why. If it's what you truly want, then you have the power within you to make it come true. But wishes that don't align with your true feelings cannot become reality.'

I looked at her in confusion. 'But I really mean it when I say I want to win the lottery.'

I knew there was no way it would happen, but who didn't want to win the lottery?

Venus grumbled, crossing her arms. 'When you say you want to win the lottery, you're basically saying you want money, right?'

I smiled awkwardly at hearing it put so frankly, but nodded. When I did, Venus drew a playing card – a diamond – from her pocket and said, 'Money is essentially a ticket you can use to exchange for experiences.'

She flipped the card over to show an image of a young man setting out on a journey.

'For example, you can exchange your ticket – money – for the experience of travelling, or the experience of eating delicious food, or the experience of buying a house.'

Venus placed the card on the bar and then looked back at me.

'I believe the stars of the Universe are always supporting people who want to experience something. That's why they're prepared to give out a ticket specifically for whatever it is you want to experience, in the form of money. But if you go to them and say, "Just give me a ticket, I don't care what it's for," they'll be confused, right? They couldn't give it to you even if they wanted to. And that's what you're saying when you say you want to win the lottery.'

I was finally starting to understand her point.

'I suppose I want to win the lottery because I've decided I want money, but I haven't decided what for.'

'There are, of course, people in the world who truly want to experience winning the lottery. They have the power to make that come true because it's their true wish. But when you say it, it's not because it's your true wish but because you're avoiding looking at yourself.'

'Avoiding?' I said, my eyes wide with indignation.

She chuckled and held up a finger. 'Now that we've established money is a ticket you exchange for an experience, let me ask you again: what experience do you wish for?'

I went silent. I wanted a flat. I wanted not to have to work. But I knew they weren't my true wishes. It was avoidance again.

What do I truly want?

The wheels of my mind turned. And, eventually, I settled on something modest.

'I want to be a permanent employee.'

'At your current job?' asked the man sitting next to me.

I looked away, once again struggling to find the right words.

No, not at my current job.

To be honest, I didn't mind where, so long as I was permanent. But what did that mean? I didn't even really know. My brow furrowed in thought.

Finally, deep inside me, I caught a faint glimpse of truth. My initial reaction was rejection, a refusal to accept it. I shook my head, trying to clear away the stubbornness, and said, 'No, that wasn't my true wish either. I . . . want to be needed.'

Saying it out loud made it feel real, and the corners of my eyes grew hot.

'By whom?' asked the man.

I laughed at myself. 'No one in particular.'

Society. Work. A person. I wanted to be needed by someone, anyone.

'Why do you want to be needed?' asked Venus gently.

My dad died when I was eight. It was Christmas Eve and snow was falling. He was on his way home from work, rushing to go and buy me a Christmas present. He had to hurry because the toy shop was about to close. But as he crossed an intersection without traffic lights, his car spun out of control and flipped over. He died almost instantly. No one ever said it, but everyone was thinking it: he died because of me.

His death turned our lives upside down. Now a single mother, Mum had to get a job. She'd come home every day looking exhausted. Every time I saw that face, I felt I was to blame. That's why I tried to be as cheerful as I could at home. I worked so hard to be the 'good kid' who was never needy, who helped out around the house.

I wasn't at all happy when my mum remarried, but I put on a huge show of being happy. I pretended to love my new dad, pretended I thought my new little brother was the cutest in the world. But I knew deep down that I was just a nuisance. Both my mum and my new dad would urge me to come and visit and show them my cheery face. But I knew it was just lip service. The truth was that neither of them needed me.

That's why I at least wanted to be needed at work, but I'd always been the 'unchosen'. I'd tried so hard to find a permanent position and failed. I started temping and put more than 100 per cent into every place I was assigned to, but none of them ever made me permanent. Every time it happened, I'd feel like I was being branded as someone unnecessary, no matter where I went.

'That's why I want to be chosen. I want to be needed.'

My nose tingled as I spoke. I looked down, then heard something being plunked in front of me. It was a white plate holding a delicious-looking, dome-shaped dark brown dessert. Atop it was a golden chestnut, circled by sparkling gold powder, chopped nuts and dried strawberries.

'I'm sorry for the wait. Here is your New Moon Mont Blanc,' said the master cat with a smile.

'New moon?' I asked. I looked up at the sky and saw a clear, shining moon.

'Tonight isn't a new moon, but we set aside the best chestnuts, let them soak in the invisible light of the new moon and then used them to make this Mont Blanc.'

I rubbed my eyes before looking at the master. 'Does the light of a new moon make them taste better?'

'The new moon has the power to make wishes come true. This dish holds the hope that you will come to realise what your true wish is and that it will come true.'

I smiled weakly at him. 'Thank you. I actually just realised what it is.'

I want to be needed by someone.

That was my wish.

Venus looked at the master bashfully when I said that.

'That may of course be the case,' he said, 'but I think you have a bigger, more important wish.' Venus nodded in agreement. I frowned, not understanding what they meant.

'Your Moon sign is Pisces, meaning it may be difficult for you to realise what your true wish is right now,' the master said.

'I'm a Pisces? No, I was born in December. I'm a Sagittarius.'

The man next to me chuckled at how flustered I was. 'Should we set that aside for now and eat?' he asked.

'We probably should . . .' I looked over at him.

In front of him were some perfectly round chocolates and a coffee.

'This is a Black Hole Chocolate Sphere,' explained

the master. 'We took a black hole – which absorbs all light – and turned it into chocolate.'

'Mmm, I'm excited. Thank you, Master,' said the man. He took a sip of his coffee and said, 'That's good.' His eyes crinkled in a smile of true pleasure. He seemed to have really wanted a coffee. He didn't even touch the chocolates and just drank the coffee.

I thanked the master for the food before picking up my fork. The Mont Blanc was filled with air, making it soft and fluffy. It wasn't overly sweet, yet its rich flavour hit with a punch. The inside was smooth, creamy cheesecake. The slightly refreshing milky flavour offset the richness of the crème de marrons to make a harmonious combination.

'This is delicious . . . It really is wonderful,' I said. It was like a reward for the hard work I'd done.

'I'm glad you're enjoying it,' said the man kindly, and I nodded. 'You know, I've dreamed of having coffee here for a long time,' he continued.

'You wanted a coffee that badly?'

Maybe he'd given it up?

He laughed at my confused face before looking me in the eyes.

'It's because I wanted to see you again.'

'What?'

'It makes me so happy to see you, Koyuki.'

My eyes widened in shock when he said my name. I met his gaze and saw his pained smile.

'I'm sorry,' he said.

How does he know my name? Why is he apologising?

I gazed at him, flustered, but looking at him, really looking deep into his eyes, revived a long-forgotten memory.

Of course . . .

How could I have forgotten?

Something fluffy and white was falling from the sky: snow.

'Fourteen years ago today,' he said, 'I was late getting off work on Christmas Eve. But I was determined to buy you a toy on the way home. I was in a rush when I left the office, that much is true.'

My heart pounded loudly in my chest as I listened to him.

'But that's not why I flew off the road. I saw a cat that couldn't move. All I could think was how horrible it'd be if my car ran it over, so I swerved off the road. I wasn't thinking about what would happen after that, about how my action would hurt you and Mummy . . . My only redemption is that the cat lived.'

He smiled.

Oh, yeah.

In our family back then, Dad was always 'Dad'

and Mum was 'Mummy'. Even Dad called my mother 'Mummy' when I was around.

My heart was still thundering. My body was shaking, and my head felt light.

This . . . This can't be real.

My mother had taken down all my father's photos because it hurt her too much to see them. I also avoided looking at them because I blamed myself. He'd been such a kind, stylish and handsome man. I'd loved him. I'd loved him with all my heart. And I hated Christmas, the day that stole him away from me.

'From the moment you were born, I looked forward to having little dates with you once you got bigger, Koyuki, but it never happened. The accident happened before you could grow up,' he said, his voice heavy as he drank his coffee.

A lump in the back of my throat blocked words from coming out.

Those big hands, stroking my hair as he looked into my eyes. That carefree smile, like a child's, even though he was a grown adult. There was no doubt in my mind. Those features were in the memories of my father I'd locked away.

In a tiny voice, I asked, 'Is that really you, Dad?'

'I'm sorry, Koyuki. It's not your fault I died. And it wasn't the cat's fault, either. It was just something that couldn't be avoided.' His large hand cradled my head.

'No . . . No, I'm sorry,' I said. I hadn't even recognised his face when I first saw him. My body wouldn't stop shaking. My eyes were hot with tears, but they wouldn't spill out, perhaps because I was in shock.

'It's all right,' he said. 'You were still just a little girl.' As he spoke, he wrapped his scarf around my neck.

'But it's not just that. Mummy found a new husband and I . . . I pretended to be happy even though I wasn't at all happy,' I said, the words gushing out from deep inside me.

I'd always felt bad for Dad. I hid away everything to do with him despite having cherished him up until then. I welcomed a new father into my life and acted like I loved him. I never managed to forgive myself for doing that. I still felt bad for Dad, and I couldn't forgive myself for being so fake.

'It's all right, Koyuki,' said my father. 'I was watching over Mummy, seeing how hard she worked. I was happy to see her take the next step in her life.'

I still couldn't bring myself to say anything. He looked into my eyes and smiled.

'The people in this world might not truly understand what it feels like, but there's nothing that can make someone like me gone to the other world happier than seeing their family happy. I am overjoyed that Mummy has found happiness with her new husband.'

'Really?'

He nodded firmly. 'And I was so relieved when I saw he was a truly good person. He's really nice to you, too, isn't he?'

Even coming from him, I couldn't bring myself to accept it. 'It's just because he loves Mummy. He's just being considerate,' I said, but I couldn't help looking away then for having put it that way.

'Koyuki, when you were still in your mummy's belly, your due date was Christmas Day.'

I nodded. I already knew that. 'That's why you picked the name Koyuki for me before I was born, if I turned out to be a girl.'

He nodded. 'There was another name we considered.'

That part I didn't know.

'If you turned out to be a boy, I told Mummy I wanted to name you Sei. You know, written with the character for "holy".'

I looked up in shock. 'Sei . . .? Really?' That was my half-brother's name.

'Really. Your new dad accepted what Mummy and I had together and was happy to name the son he had with her Sei. He has such a big heart. That's why you don't need to worry, Koyuki. He knew what he was getting into becoming your father, and he accepted it.'

I was silent. I was lost for words. I just looked at my dad blankly.

What have I been doing this entire time?

I'd blamed myself for my father's death. I'd wanted to remember him but wouldn't let myself. I'd pretended to accept my new father but hadn't truly done so. I'd even convinced myself he was just pretending to be kind to me. None of it was the truth. How did it all get so twisted?

It had all started with my blaming myself. My eyes opened wide. I finally understood. I finally knew what my true wish was.

'To forgive myself . . .'

Tears burst from my eyes the moment I said the words.

I wasn't sad, but the dam broke and the tears came flooding out along with everything I'd kept pent up inside.

I'd been suffering for so long. I hadn't managed to forgive myself. I just kept on blaming myself. Someone like me couldn't be chosen for anything because, deep within me, I believed it wasn't right for someone like me to be chosen.

I'd rejected happiness this entire time. I'd believed

I needed to accept punishment and atone for what I'd done. I'd actually *wanted* this situation I'd found myself in where no one ever chose me for anything. It all made so much sense.

My tears wouldn't stop, as if all the pain I'd carried was now being washed away.

'I'm so glad I got to talk to you tonight, Koyuki. It's a miracle, after fourteen years,' my dad said happily. He lifted a spoonful of his Black Hole Chocolate Sphere, exclaiming at how there seemed to be glowing stars inside the round shape as he popped the spoon into his mouth. With each spoonful, his body glowed a brighter white.

'Dad!' I stood up, but his form had dissolved like melting snow, leaving behind only sparkling lights.

4

Dad.

I wiped my tears and looked up to find myself no longer in the rooftop garden. I was standing at the entrance to the Asakura Museum of Sculpture. The doors were closed. The food truck that had been parked on the grounds was gone, as were the Christmas lights.

'What . . .?'

I'd been certain the moon had been shining in the sky a moment ago, but it was now dusk.

Was I daydreaming?

'What happened?' I asked, looking around with

tears still leaking from my eyes. I wiped them away again, still disorientated. That's when I noticed the scarf hanging from my neck. I remembered my dad's smile as he wrapped it around me. My chest tightened.

I checked my phone and saw that not much time had passed since I'd left the shopping arcade. I turned on my heel and headed back the way I came.

'Um, excuse me. I was wondering if I might take you up on that offer of a Christmas cake,' I said.

The man from the association broke into a big smile at my unexpected return. 'Of course. But what changed? Did you make some plans with friends?'

'Actually, I've decided to visit my family tonight.'

I was certain they'd already have a Christmas cake, but these were relatively small. The four of us should manage to finish one off. I wanted to have a fun Christmas Eve with my mum, my little brother and my new dad.

By the time I'd collected a cake and left the shopping arcade, scattered flakes of white snow were drifting through the dark sky.

Thank you, Dad. And everyone at the Full Moon Coffee Shop.

I touched the scarf as I whispered the words to myself. I lifted my head determinedly and hurried towards the station.

Tonight was a night of miracles.

Interlude

The Christmas lights still gleamed in the rooftop garden of the Asakura Museum of Sculpture. Koyuki Suzumiya and her father had been sitting at the bar not long before, but they had left now. With the customers gone, the rooftop garden had been transformed into a party venue for the staff of the Full Moon Coffee Shop.

'Thank you, everyone, for your hard work. Let us drink a toast to a request fulfilled. Go on, have a cocktail.'

The tortoiseshell master treated the staff the same as he did customers. He didn't take their orders and instead made bespoke cocktails of his choice for each one.

'I'll pass them out, Master,' said Luna, her long black hair tied back in a ponytail as she carried the cocktails over to everyone. In the rooftop garden were the master, Luna, Mercury, Jupiter, Saturn, Uranus and me, Venus. The master waited until everyone had a drink in their hand before raising his glass in a toast.

'Unsurprisingly, old man Pluto and oddball Neptune aren't with us,' said Uranus with a grin. He was the blond one whose hair had the pink layer underneath. He sat across from the silver-haired boy, Mercury, at a small table. They were playing chess.

'They're not the sort to come to something like this,' muttered Mercury as he touched a chess piece.

'Guess not,' said Uranus. 'They are trans-Saturnians, after all.'

'That goes for you too, doesn't it?'

The trans-Saturnians were the three planets beyond Saturn: Uranus, Neptune and Pluto. The planets up to Saturn can be seen with the naked eye from Earth, but the trans-Saturnians cannot be perceived by humans, placing them within the realm of the subconsciousness.

'I am so far away I can never be reached. I'm almost like any old star in that way, but the Age of Aquarius means I've got work to do every now and then. Once all this fuss dies down, I'll go back to my typical aloof self as a trans-Saturnian.'

Uranus laughed loudly, but Mercury frowned.

'Oh, don't make that face, brother. I'm not running off right away.'

After pausing a moment, Mercury said, 'You always do things your way, don't you?'

These two people were polar opposites. Uranus was rather eccentric and Mercury level-headed and analytical, but they had similar temperaments, so they got on well. Well, they aren't actually 'people' at all. I'm only referring to them as people because they're in human form.

'Come on, hurry up and get the match underway. I'm playing Mercury next,' said a virile, red-headed young man. That was Mars. He held a Red Eye cocktail in one hand while eying the unmoving chess pieces with irritation. He could be a bit impatient at times, but he was also proactive and straightforward. And manly. Though there was always something boyish about him too.

Someone like him was bound to attract me.

'V, has Mars caught your eye again?' came a teasing voice from behind, making me jump. I turned around to see a plump, cheery, middle-aged woman: Jupiter. She had a Margarita in one hand as she gave me a playful look.

'Cut it out, Jupiter!' I said, my burning cheeks sending me in a tizzy.

'You mustn't tease the children like that,' said a sombre gentleman – Saturn – chiding Jupiter. He was drinking his gin and tonic at the bar.

'Oh, I'm sorry, dear,' said Jupiter. 'Anyway, Saturn, V, did the two of you know that . . .'

'Even you are calling me "Saturn" rather than "Cronus" now, Jupiter?' Saturn's face contorted in discomfort, but Jupiter absentmindedly said, 'What's wrong with it? It's cute,' before continuing. The two of them were utterly different people, but they both acknowledged each other as greatly powerful.

'Did you know that, just as flowers have a language, drinks have a language, too?' said Jupiter. 'The gin and tonic you're drinking means "strong will". It's just like the master to pick the perfect cocktail for you.'

'Hmm,' said Saturn, impressed. His mood seemed to improve.

My face lit up when I heard that, and I leaned towards Jupiter. 'Hey, I have a Wine Cooler. What does that mean?'

This Wine Cooler was a mixture of rosé wine, orange juice, grenadine and white curaçao, shaken. It was a vibrant and delicious drink.

Jupiter giggled and said, 'That one means "steal my heart".'

'Huh?'

'I'm not the only one teasing you, V. Though, when the master does it, it's less teasing and more giving you a little push.'

'But . . .' I stammered, unable to find the right words as I looked over in Mars's direction. I felt like he'd been glancing in my direction every once in a while, and our eyes seemed about to . . .

'Ack!'

I tore my eyes way and turned, bringing the drink to my mouth to distract from my flushing cheeks. Jupiter let out a heartfelt sigh as if to say, 'Oh, how cute.' Saturn gave an exasperated shrug.

'That's right, V,' said Jupiter. 'Tonight is Christmas Eve. You should make the most of the atmosphere and take the next step in your relationship with Mars. Go give him your Wine Cooler and tell him this is how you feel.'

'I couldn't possibly!' My eyes darted around as Saturn let out a monumental sigh.

'I disagree with Jupiter. I can't say I approve of advancing romantic relationships by allowing yourself to get swept up in passing moods.'

'Oh, what's wrong with it?' pouted Jupiter as she spread her arms wide. 'Just look! Christmas cheer is giving love a little helping hand. It's rooting for lovers.'

'If two people are truly of the same mind, then they

need not be swept away before acting. They can simply follow the proper procedures.'

'Come on. Love *is* being swept away.'

'No, it's . . .'

'I imagine you're the sort who prefers arranged marriages over marrying for love.'

'An arranged marriage begins with the parents introducing candidates they approve of. If a couple then finds they agree, I can't see what could possibly be better.'

'I cannot believe it. There are no words to describe how unromantic that is.'

'Not all arranged marriages are lacking in love.'

'I guess not.'

I grimaced with exasperation as I listened to their argument. Despite their respect for one another, they were polar opposites. At times like this, they were utterly incompatible. In an attempt to change the subject, I pointed to Jupiter's cocktail and asked, 'You're drinking a Margarita, right?'

'That's right.'

'What does that mean?'

'The Margarita means "quiet love",' she said, bringing a hand to her chest.

'That doesn't seem very suited to you. You're always running your mouth,' said Saturn smoothly.

'How rude.' Jupiter pouted. 'I give love to so many without ever saying anything. Like earlier, with Koyuki's father.'

That made me think back to the customers from this evening: Koyuki and her father. Emotion welled in my chest as I thought of the father continuing to watch over his daughter in silence. And yet there was something I still didn't get.

'Jupiter, I didn't really understand what the master said to Koyuki.'

'What was that?'

'About her true wish,' I said, and repeated the master's message: '*Your Moon sign is Pisces, meaning it may be difficult for you to realise what your true wish is right now.*'

'I don't understand,' I continued, 'how having the Moon in Pisces makes it hard for someone to realise what their true wish is.' The minute the question left my mouth I heard a beautiful voice ring out behind me, as clear as a bell: 'It's because the Moon is immature.'

I turned to see Luna. Her cocktail was a Violet Fizz – a gorgeous-looking drink the same colour as her eyes. She'd let her hair down, perhaps because she'd finished serving the drinks. Her lustrous, perfectly straight black locks gleamed in the moonlight.

'Luna!' I cried. I'd always admired her. She was

mysterious and somewhat aloof. But there was something not quite right about what she'd just said.

'The Moon is immature?' I asked, cocking my head.

Luna nodded, tucking her long hair behind her ear. 'In the astrological Ages of Man, the Moon represents life from birth until around age seven.'

I'd heard the master tell customers their planetary phase and astrological Ages of Man before. It all started with the Moon.

'The Moon points to the period from when people are born until they begin to develop their own self, meaning the Moon is their bare, unadulterated self. It's a bit like instinct, undeveloped and unrefined. In other words, it's immature.'

I listened to Luna without saying anything. It was true that humans were so immature from birth until around the age of seven that you couldn't even let them out of your sight.

'A person's Sun sign is the face they show to the world, right?' continued Luna. 'Most people have mastered the use of their Sun sign because they've spent so long bringing it to the fore as their prominent self. Take Aries, for example. No matter how hard they try, a person with an Aries Moon sign could never outcompete a person with an Aries Sun sign in an area that uses that constellation's abilities.'

That much was true. The Sun sign, as a person's external self, was like a warrior fighting on the front lines throughout a person's life, while the Moon sign was more like a cloistered lady.

'Which is why it's not uncommon for people to develop a complex around their Moon sign. The Aries Moon sign person, for example, is likely to feel inferior to the Aries Sun sign person.'

That seemed logical enough. 'Because the Moon sign person has the same ability, but they're not able to wield it as effectively as the Sun sign person,' I said, and Luna nodded.

'Koyuki, the girl who was here a little while ago, has Pisces as her Moon sign, right? In fact, that reminds me, the other customer we had not long ago also had a Pisces Moon sign.'

I looked up, remembering. 'That's right. Junko. Her Moon sign was Pisces.'

And that had happened two weeks ago.

Chapter 3

A Bond from a Previous Life and Sparkler Iced Tea

Junko Ichihara

線香花火のアイスティー

1

People often say the city seems to come alive in December. Iias, the shopping centre near my home, grew more and more decorated with each passing day as Christmas drew nearer. My daughter, Ayu, and I had stopped by the food hall on our way home from a parent-teacher meeting. There were a lot of children in school uniforms, despite it being the middle of a weekday. Maybe school had let out earlier than usual.

When I was a student, my friends and I would hang out in a fast-food joint and chat endlessly. But now? I looked down at the girl beside me whom I loved with all my heart.

Thanks to her friends, Ayu, who was in her first

year of primary school, had got it into her head that she wanted one of the free toys the doughnut shop gave away with the kids' orders. The toy was from a children's TV programme called *Shooting Star Angels*. It was sort of like *Power Rangers* for girls. A team of three iconic girls used the power of the sun, the moon and the stars to fight an evil organisation. The toy you got was one of the wands they used, and you had a choice of three: Sun, Moon or Star. I really liked the Moon wand with its crescent shape on top, but Ayu chose the Star wand. She was still holding it, her face beaming.

'Ayu, don't play around too long. Finish your Saturn doughnut,' I said, rubbing her back.

She nodded and picked up the doughnut with both tiny hands, bringing it to her tiny mouth. It was all so very cute, but at this pace it would also take her quite a while to finish eating. It might be a kid's order, but it was still a lot of food for my daughter. I'd probably end up finishing the doughnut.

Basically, there were far too many hurdles in the way of maintaining your diet when you were raising a child. And I'd been hit with a shock only last night when I'd stepped on the scales . . .

But it is what it is. I imagined I managed to shrug these things off because I wasn't a young mother. I'd only become pregnant with Ayu after going through a long process of fertility treatment and giving up. That was why I was quite a bit older than the mothers of the other children in Ayu's class.

I saw those young mothers growing irritated or panicked at their child's actions, while I felt it was only natural for them to be that way. If I had been in my twenties or even my early thirties, I would probably have nagged Ayu to eat faster. An older woman's body may find pregnancies hard to bear, but her mind is better prepared.

Once I saw Ayu was eating, I let my eyes lazily drift over the store. I couldn't help staring at a group of secondary-school girls carrying the same toys as Ayu.

'No way,' said one. 'You went with Sun? I got Moon.'

'Of course. Sun is my girl.'

Apparently, my daughter's favourite programme was popular with the older girls too. Thinking about it, I realised even adults could find the show interesting. It was about girls who had served the *kami* – the sacred beings of the Shinto religion – during Japan's Age of the Gods, but were now reborn in the modern era. It drew on beliefs of reincarnation and Western astrology. The script was actually written by a woman whose work had been incredibly popular a while ago. She fell off the cultural radar but then had a resurgence and was now working on the show. I was fairly certain she was from my generation, or maybe just a tad younger.

I picked up my phone, trying to remember her name. I typed the programme's title into a search engine and soon found her: Mizuki Serikawa.

'That's right. Mizuki Serikawa,' I said.

I found an interview with Serikawa and the show's producer, Akari Nakayama. *Shooting Star Angels* was a joint effort between the two women.

'Mizuki Serikawa. That name brings back a lot of memories.'

I had loved her dramas. I used to watch them all the time. Serikawa had disappeared for a while, but continued garnering praise for the scenes she wrote for mobile games. Considering how much of a hot topic the children's programme had become, I thought it was safe to say Serikawa was back in the game.

'What're you looking at, Mum?' asked Ayu. I showed her my phone.

'This woman, Mizuki Serikawa, is the person who wrote the story for *Shooting Star Angels*. And this one here, Akari Nakayama, is the one who made it.'

'What's the difference between writing and making a TV programme?'

'Er, well, if it's only written, it'd just stay a book,

right? You wouldn't be able to watch it on TV unless someone turned it into a TV programme.'

'Huh,' said Ayu, sounding impressed. 'They're both amazing.'

'You're right. They're both amazing.'

I felt pride at how well Serikawa was doing, since we were of the same generation. I realised from reading the interview that she was single, and part of me wondered if she was truly okay with being unmarried and childless. But it wasn't a concern I should have had. I chided myself the moment the thought popped in my head. *No. Don't repeat the things Dad used to say.*

My father had an old-fashioned set of values, typical of the Shōwa era in which he had grown up: women have no use for education or jobs. They should marry early and have children. He'd always say things like that to me. I'd even heard that my name, Junko, written with the characters for 'pure' and 'child', came from the idea that women should be innocent and submissive.

My father had had high hopes for my younger brother Jiro, who was clever and obedient. But Jiro had cracked under that intense pressure. It happened just after I'd left for university, when Jiro was still in secondary school.

That was what made me cut ties with my father. It was easy enough, considering I'd just moved into the university dorms. I hardly ever went back home and instead asked my mum to visit if I wanted to see her. I only returned home when I knew my father wasn't going to be there.

'And that's why . . .' I whispered.

That's why I couldn't be there when my dog, Rin, whom I loved so much, died. Remembering that day made my nose tingle and my eyes grow hot. Some people might say she was just a dog, but it wasn't that simple: Rin was family.

Rin – a mixed breed that looked like a Shiba Inu – had the most adorable round eyes and always looked at me with such a happy face. Whenever I'd had a hard time at school or I was down because my father was angry at me, she'd come over without me even having to say anything. I still hadn't forgotten what it felt like to stroke her.

'Our dog will be coming home soon,' said Ayu, shocking me out of my reverie.

'Oh, yeah. That's right.'

We'd decided to adopt a dog, but she hadn't yet come home. There were all sorts of procedures that had to be followed first.

'Have you picked a name?' I asked.

She groaned. 'I've thought a lot about it, but I still can't decide.'

'What sort of names are you considering?'

'Maybe something like Jennifer or Jasmine?'

'They sound like princess names.'

'Yeah, but I don't know if she'll like a long name.'

'Maybe not.'

'What was the dog you had a long time ago called, Mum?'

Her question shocked me. It was like she'd been reading my mind. Ayu had mysterious moments like that.

After a while, I said, 'Her name was Rin.'

'Did you name her?'

'I did.'

'Why'd you pick Rin?'

I faltered at the unexpected question. 'Why did I?'

'Was it from the ringing sound bells make?'

'No, it wasn't a bell . . .'

Now that she'd brought it up, I actually couldn't remember. I wrapped my arms around myself and searched deep within my memories until I found the me from all that time ago.

I had been big into divination and good-luck charms at the time. That was it. In primary school, I was obsessed with a manga featuring rebirth. It was a human-centric drama in which the characters were reincarnated and met each other again.

I'd been so happy when we got a dog. But my father had always been against it. As absurd as it was, he'd said something horrible the day the dog came: 'Dogs don't live long. She'll die soon, and you'll just be sad.' I was really hurt by his heartless comment, even angry at him for saying such a thing when I was so happy. I had retorted in a quiet voice so he couldn't hear: 'Fine, it doesn't matter. We'll be reborn and find each other again.' That was why I named her Rin. It was from the Japanese word *rinne*, meaning the cycle of reincarnation.

I told Ayu how I came up with the name, leaving out the bit about what my father had said, and she giggled, her eyes sparkling. 'Can I name the new puppy Rin too?'

'What? Oh, well, that would be fine.'

'All right! Her name's Rin!'

I was struck with an odd emotion as I watched Ayu squirm with joy. I'd named my childhood dog Rin in the hope we'd meet again, even if only in another life. Over thirty years had passed since then. I was now a parent myself, and our new dog had just been named Rin. It occurred to me then that our new Rin was also a Shiba Inu, just like my old Rin. Maybe it really was her.

As I was sinking into that dreamy thought, my phone pinged with a message. I tapped the screen assuming it was my husband, but I was surprised to see it was my brother. That little brother who had cracked in secondary school under my father's pressure was now over forty years old. He was a fine adult. For Mum's sake, Jiro had gone through the motions of apologising, but he and Dad never truly reconciled. I doubted they ever would. My brother resented my father, and my father didn't accept my brother.

My father had always been fond of Jiro. As a child, I'd often been envious when my father lavished him with praise. And yet, I'd also been aware of how much pressure my brother was enduring. I saw how often he would grit his teeth and clench his fists whenever my father said something ridiculous or raised his voice. I waited in a cold sweat, wondering when he would use those fists in revolt.

He eventually reached his limit and exploded, and the bomb he dropped was enormous. Our family unit was broken from that moment on. My brother was never at home, and my mother hid out at our grandmother's. Before then, I'd assumed Jiro would end up in some safe, high-flying career, but he was now in the beauty industry.

My brother may have been the trigger that resulted in the family's fracturing, but I empathised because I too had been on the verge of exploding on our father. I didn't resent Jiro for it, but he did seem to feel guilty for how things went down. He distanced himself from the family so as not to cause any more trouble. I only heard from him rarely as a result.

Had something happened?

Worried, I checked the message:

Hey sis, long time no chat. I got married.

I shrieked the moment I read that utterly unexpected sentence.

'What's wrong?' Ayu asked, looking up at me. I rubbed her back and told her it was nothing before leaning my head on my fist. I just couldn't believe he was married. Even if he had been in a relationship, I would have assumed they'd cohabit forever without getting married. This had the potential to turn into another huge mess if my father heard.

I let out a little sigh. That's when Ayu said, 'I'm done.' She'd polished off the doughnut before I'd realised it and was now looking up at me with pride.

'And what do we say when we finish eating?' I asked.

'Thank you for the food!' She put her hands together and bowed her head, then bounced to her feet. I picked up the tray, happening to overhear something as I did. 'So, earlier, I got a past-life reading from the fortune teller. She's *so* pretty,' one of the secondary-school girls was saying.

Maybe I'd gravitated towards their conversation because I'd always liked that past-life stuff. I now was, of course, a perfectly well-grown adult in both body and mind, so I knew it was all nonsense. But I was a little curious when I heard there was a fortune teller in the shopping centre, so I continued listening in.

One of the girls was leaning in, pressing the other to give up the details. 'Were you a noblewoman during the French Revolution?'

'Or royalty in ancient Egypt?' asked another.

I couldn't help smiling as, out of the corner of my eye, I watched the girls edging closer to their friend. During my school days, I'd also done the past-life divination quizzes in those fortune-telling magazines and was always happy to find out I had been a European noblewoman or Arabian royalty.

It wasn't as if everyone could have been royalty or nobility, though.

The fortune teller would have, of course, asked this schoolgirl all sorts of psychologically leading questions to mine her for information. It's a technique called cold reading. The fortune teller would then hazard a guess at what sort of past life their customer was hoping for and serve up an answer that satisfied their expectations. There was no way to confirm your past life, so it didn't matter if they were right or wrong.

So I wasn't expecting the first girl to roll her eyes as she continued with, 'It wasn't like that. She just told me what I've brought with me from my previous life. And she didn't even let me pay her.'

'What do you mean what you brought from your previous life? What's that?'

I too wondered about that as I returned the tray and left the food hall with Ayu.

After walking a short while, I saw a sign at the side of the hallway that said FORTUNE TELLING. It listed types of divination I was familiar with – palm reading, name divination, astrology – but also one I didn't recognise: past-life power.

'Mum, that's the princess from Tokyo.'

Ayu's wild statement left me blinking in bewilderment. She was pointing at the fortune teller. I reminded her it was rude to point, but when I looked at the woman, I understood.

The woman sitting at the booth looked European, with the kind of hair that is so pale it is nearly see-through – platinum blonde, maybe – and skin the colour of porcelain. She looked like a film star, with features so perfect she might have just stepped out of a religious painting. I also felt as if I'd seen her somewhere before, so perhaps she actually was an actress of some sort.

'She really does look like a princess,' I said.

'She doesn't just look like one. She is the princess from Tokyo.'

'What do you mean, the princess from Tokyo?'

'She was at the castle place I went to with Auntie Sato.'

I guessed Ayu meant Château Restaurant at Yebisu Garden Place.

'And she was also at the park where we met our new dog,' continued Ayu.

'Ah.' The light bulb went on. 'You're right. She was one of the musicians. Maybe she's an event planner like Aunt Sato.'

'Event planner?'

As we were talking, the woman looked up with a slight smile – she must have overheard – and gestured for us to come over. Ayu's face lit up and she hurried over to the woman. 'Hello!' she said cheerfully, and the woman's eyes crinkled in a smile.

'Hello, miss. It's lovely to see you again. Please, sit down.'

'Okay.'

My eyes widened when Ayu plopped herself without hesitation into the chair across from the woman.

'Would you like a reading?' asked the woman softly as she looked up at me. I hesitated. She noticed and quickly continued, 'I don't take payment.' But that still didn't mean I could trust her completely.

'Erm, about this past-life divination . . .' I said, still feeling suspicious.

She quickly shook her head. 'Actually, it's past-life *power* – not past-life divination.'

'Past-life power?' I asked, puzzled.

She chuckled. 'It's from astrology. Everyone has some power they've carried over from their past life. I take a look at what that is.'

'What's my past-life power?' asked Ayu innocently.

'One moment.' The woman took out a pocket watch, which she touched to Ayu's forehead. She popped open the lid to project a horoscope.

20/12/2014, 10:30:36. Ayu's date and time of birth.

'The characteristics, gifts and abilities you are born with are in fact things you carried over from your previous life,' said the woman. 'We can see this on the left-hand edge of this circle, which is your Ascendant, sometimes abbreviated "ASC". It's this line at the beginning of the first house that separates the first house from the twelfth. Ayu, your Sun sign is Sagittarius and your Moon sign is also Sagittarius. Your Ascendant is Pisces. That's what you've carried over from your previous life.'

'What does having a Pisces Ascendant mean?' I

asked, my face screwed up because I didn't understand what she was talking about, but I always did like this sort of thing. I realised then I was leaning in towards her.

'It means Ayu innately has the power of Pisces.'

'What's the power of Pisces?'

'Vibrant imagination, tolerance towards others, the ability to soothe others and a strong sixth sense. Those are the sorts of characteristics Pisces has, so they are Ayu's past-life powers.'

I gasped.

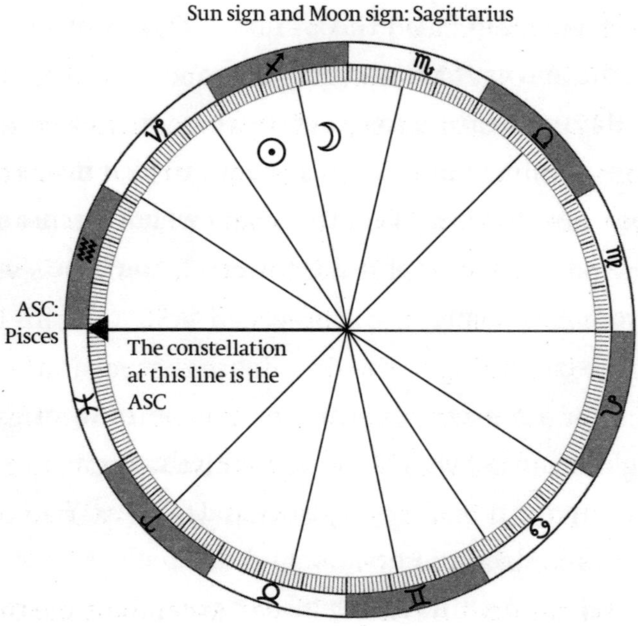

The woman continued. 'These are the things Ayu picked up throughout her past life. That's why she has the innate ability to do them well, without having to try. They're essentially the talents she was born with.'

I caught myself letting out an impressed sigh.

The woman looked at me and picked up the watch. 'Would you also like a look?'

'Er, yes. If you don't mind.'

My shoulders scrunched and my body tensed. As the woman laid the watch over my forehead, I felt a soft warmth spread from between my eyes across my brow. Once again, the watch projected an image of a horoscope.

'Now, Mum,' said the woman. 'Your Sun sign is Gemini and your Moon sign is Pisces.'

Having heard about Ayu's horoscope, I thought Pisces was incredible, so I was happy to hear it was my Moon sign, but I wasn't entirely sure what that meant.

'And as for your past-life power . . . You have Virgo as your Ascendant.'

'Virgo?'

I had a hard time forming an image of what that might mean as I wasn't familiar with that sign.

'Virgo is the goddess of justice and fairness. You have talent and strong observational skills. You're capable of analysing anything calmly and of providing generous support to others from behind the scenes. You're really quite wonderful, actually.'

I blushed at the intense praise. In truth, I did often support people from behind the scenes.

'On the other hand,' she continued, 'there's a side of you that's very delicate and easily wounded.'

That was also true. I went silent, falling deep into thought. The woman looked at me uneasily.

'Is something wrong?' she asked.

'It's incredible,' I said.

'I agree. Astrology is incredible.' She suddenly sat up straight in pride, but then her shoulders slumped. 'But I'm still just learning. I have a long way to go. That's why I'm doing this – reading as many natal charts as I can and learning from them.'

So that's why she was offering her services for free.

'Technically,' she said, 'the Ascendant also shows up in other places, not just in the abilities you were born with. It shows in people's first impressions of you and in your external appearance. It's actually my astrology teacher who interprets Ascendants as the characteristics you carry over from your previous life.'

She cradled the pocket watch in her palm as if it were a precious object.

'Is there a benefit to knowing your past-life power?' I asked. She stopped and blinked.

'Of course. Everything, even fortune, begins with knowing yourself.'

I gave a vague sound of agreement. A part of me felt as if it understood, but another didn't.

'Let's use a video game as an example. If life is a role-playing game, your Ascendant is the equipment you start out with. You haven't been trained to use the weapon, but you innately know how. You set out on a journey in which you are the main character with that weapon in hand.'

I visualised an RPG game screen, with music playing in the background.

'Don't you think you'd struggle a bit if you didn't even know what your weapon was?' she asked.

'Yes, you would struggle.' My expression had turned serious as I spoke. The woman chuckled at that.

'If you know what it is, you can use it more effectively. It'll make your journey easier.'

'And that's your Ascendant?'

She nodded before continuing. 'But while you might use that weapon for a while, your battles evolve as you grow up. You move on to the next level in the game, and the weapon you've been using might not be as effective as it once was. You'll have to either train and hone your skills with that weapon or pick up a new one.'

I nodded along, finding the metaphor easy to follow.

'Meaning, in my case, I need to train and hone my Virgo power.'

'That's right. But there are some situations in which that might not be true. It's obviously a wonderful thing to hone your power from your previous life, but, sometimes, people become trapped in their past-life power, leaving them unable to move.'

'What do you mean?'

'For example, take someone with a Capricorn Ascendant. Capricorn is pragmatic, serious and a hard worker – quite the appropriate sign for a Japanese person, really. They lived their previous life that way, but are reborn with the desire to live like Pisces – dreamy and whimsical. But their inherited Capricorn ways tell them they can't be such a softy, which restricts them from living the life they want. They become conflicted . . . It's something you see happen sometimes.'

I wasn't entirely unfamiliar with that sort of conflict either.

'Your Ascendant just represents the starter equipment you're born with. It doesn't have to be the overarching theme of your current life,' she said.

I nodded emphatically, feeling like this sort of thing did happen quite often. An image of my brother appeared in the back of my mind. Maybe he'd always been dragged down by his Ascendant, so he repressed it.

'If someone did end up in that sort of situation, like in the Capricorn example, what should they do?' I asked.

'The most important thing is for them to know themselves. They should constantly ask themselves how they want to live their life, this life. Have a meeting of sorts with themselves to hammer things out.'

'A meeting with themselves?' A smile grew on my face.

'And if the conclusion of that meeting is that they want to live their life as free as a fish in the sea, then they can decide to live like that. But they might also decide that, since they were born with the tools of Capricorn, they may as well use them when interacting with others.'

'Which is why I don't necessarily have to hone my Virgo abilities.'

'Exactly.'

'But what if your meeting with yourself comes to the wrong conclusion?'

She looked taken aback by my question, as if it was utterly incomprehensible. 'It can't be wrong.'

'What?'

'Everyone, each and every single person, holds the Universe in their hands.' She smiled awkwardly at the suddenly religious turn of phrase before pursing her lips and saying, 'It's just the way it is, don't you see?

It's like this: there are three of us standing here, in the exact same place, but each of us is looking at something different. You're the only one who sees the sights you do. The Universe around you is for no one but you.'

That much did ring true, to me at least.

'You are a Universe, and the stars will lend their power to what you've decided on. You may struggle and wander, but you could never be wrong.'

'And what if you don't want to struggle or wander . . .?' I asked quietly.

She chuckled. 'Then you must simply decide that. The stars may light your path, but you're the one who decides where you go.'

'Huh.' I felt the tension ease from my shoulders. 'You know . . . Astrology is fun. You've piqued my interest.'

She smiled. 'I'm glad.' And she really did look glad.

Having come to the end of our past-life power reading, Ayu and I thanked the woman and left the fortune-telling corner. It had been very different from what I'd expected from a past-life divination, but I felt satisfied.

I'm glad I let her look.

I tried to pay her a little something because I was so happy with the reading, but she refused with a smile.

We left the shopping centre and were getting into our car in the car park when my phone vibrated in my pocket, almost as if it had been waiting for the right moment. I checked it to find my mother was ringing me. She was probably flustered after hearing about my brother's marriage and wanted to talk.

'Hi, Mum,' I answered the phone.

'Junko?' she replied, sounding gloomy. She must be worried about the next storm that was going to sweep through our family.

'Mum . . .' I started, trying to think of what to say, but I couldn't finish before she said the unimaginable.

'Your dad collapsed this morning. He's in hospital.'

2

After that call from my mother, Ayu and I set off for my family home in Kamakura. My husband couldn't take the time off work, and I'm not that good a driver, so I decided we'd take the train, setting off from Tsukuba Station and then changing in Kitasenju, Shinagawa and Fujisawa. It was quite a journey, taking around two and a half hours.

I had considered leaving Ayu with my husband's parents because she was still too young for this sort of trip, but she refused, insisting she wanted to come with me. I eventually caved.

She usually listened to me. This was the first time she wouldn't back down. I wondered if perhaps she'd sensed, being such a perceptive child, that my father didn't have long left.

'This is my first time going to Grandma's house in Kamakura,' Ayu said, her eyes gleaming with joy as she looked out of the window.

'I took you once when you were a baby,' I said.

Despite cutting ties with my father, I had gone home a few times, though only when he wasn't there. All those times had been with my husband, and he'd driven us there. I hadn't gone by train since I was single.

'Really? Did I meet Kamakura Grandpa?' she asked, shooting a spike of pain through my heart.

She'd never once met my father, her grandfather. Whatever my reasons, it was true that I had kept his granddaughter from him. I found my hands clenching into balls as feelings of remorse grew inside me. Ayu seemed to forget her own question and returned to looking happily out the window.

I'm sorry, I whispered internally. If I had truly had her best interests at heart, shouldn't I have let them meet?

No. That was impossible.

There was a reason I couldn't even consider the possibility.

*

My memories from the day our family shattered were still vivid. And yet, the images appeared in faded sepia tones. It was a very odd sensation.

I'd gone off to university a month earlier and hadn't entirely adjusted to life in the dorms. One day, my mother asked me to come home. She was very worried about how I was settling into my new life, whether there was anything I needed or was struggling with, so she, my father and I went to a large shopping centre to buy some things. She'd asked him to take us there in the car, but he was in a terrible mood so he said, 'I can't be bothered to go shopping. You two hurry up. I'll wait in the car.'

And he did. He spent the entire time out in the car park, waiting.

My mother and I bought all sorts of things I only realised I needed once I'd started living my new life. Time flew by without us realising. When we got back to the car, my father was livid. He kept shouting, 'What took you so long?' and 'Women!'

It was a tense ride the whole way home. I sat in the back seat with my hands balled into fists.

This is the last time, I thought. *This is the last time I spend time with him. I'm done. I'm at my limit. I'm not coming home, not even after I move out of the dorms. I'll only come when he's not here. I don't want to see him again.*

The words played over and over in my mind, like an incantation for a spell.

That was the mood when we got home. And there are some moments in life when the timing couldn't possibly be any worse.

My father didn't park in our driveway. I imagine my mother had been trying to ease the oppressive tension in the car when she suggested we have a barbecue in the driveway later, so he parked down the road. If we'd parked in the driveway that day as we usually did, my brother, who was home, would have heard the engine. He probably never imagined that we might arrive at the house on foot.

When we walked in, he was alone in the Japanese-style sitting room connected to the family room. He was wearing my white dress, appraising himself in the full-length mirror.

We were shocked by the sight.

My brother was shocked, too. He gaped at us when we appeared, his eyes wide.

And the moment my father saw him, without uttering a word, he struck him. Following the dull thud of that strike, my brother fell to his knees. Blood dripped from his nose, staining my white dress and the tatami mats red.

'Are you some kind of damned pervert?' our father howled as he grabbed my brother by the collar.

The next moment, once again without a word, my brother shoved him away with all his might, easily sending him tumbling to the floor. That also shocked me. We'd always perceived our father as this person of ultimate strength. But at some point, my brother had grown strong enough to push him over with ease.

Our father sat on the floor, flabbergasted by his son's first show of resistance.

His face swollen and with tears in his eyes, my brother shouted, 'Yeah, Dad, I've always been an *onē* !'*

I held my head in my hand, remembering it.

Things got worse afterwards. Our father shouted at my brother, telling him to get out. I turned on him and started shouting too. 'You're horrible, Dad! How could you do something so horrible? I hate you! Jiro and I have been putting up with you for so long!'

But even that didn't faze him. He turned to me, and it felt as if there was a monster looking at me and shouting, 'You can get out too! Don't ever come back. Don't think I'll keep paying your tuition. You can drop out and get yourself a job!'

I couldn't breathe when he said drop out. He was always doing that, always hitting someone's weak

* Translator's Note: *Onē* is a Japanese term for men who use feminine speech or fashion styles. They are not necessarily gay or trans, but are often assumed to be.

point and trying to take control. The problem was, he was right. My parents were paying my way through university. I could probably pay my tuition if I got a part-time job, but I wouldn't immediately be able to repay him for the money he'd spent on my fees so far.

'Fine!' I shouted. 'I will! I'll just drop out and get a job!'

At this point, I was simply fighting fire with fire.

In the end, a tearful Mum stepped in to mediate. We came to an agreement: I would be responsible for paying a portion of my tuition so I wouldn't have to drop out.

How many years ago was that?

Time had stopped because I hadn't seen my father since then. Anger surged inside me when I remembered that day. I'd believed our ties were forever cut and I no longer needed a father in my life. I never thought that would change. And yet, I couldn't help feeling conflicted when I thought about my father dying with things as they were.

3

Two hours and a bit after pulling out of Tsukuba Station, we arrived at Fujisawa Station and changed onto the Enoshima Electric Railway, which we rode for about fifteen minutes before arriving at Kamakura Kokomae, the station closest to my family's home.

'I haven't used this station in so long,' I said. It was a small, utterly ordinary, unmanned place with a single platform. The view from that platform, however, was stunning. The ocean was right in front of you, spreading out panoramically. This view was famous, so famous that Kamakura Kokomae was even named one of the Top 100 Stations in the Kanto region.

It was a familiar sight to someone like me who'd

been born, raised and lived here until secondary school. I liked it, of course, but I didn't understand why people came from far and wide to see this tiny station.

Until now. Now I understood how they felt. It had been so long since I'd looked out over this ocean, and its beauty and vastness overwhelmed me until I choked up.

A tiny train ran along the track, hugging the coastline. The place still existed. It was still breathing. It seemed like a miracle. Ayu let out a gasp and spread her arms wide in overwhelming emotion. 'The ocean goes on forever.'

She'd been full of energy at the beginning of the trip but had started dozing off partway through. The view had washed away the remnants of fatigue and returned a sparkle to her eye. I was happy to see her enjoying herself. And it seemed I liked this view even more than I thought I did. I felt the corners of my eyes grow warm with tears and, to distract myself, I took Ayu's hand to start walking away.

'Let's get going,' I said, and Ayu skipped along next to me. We came to a place where we could see what was behind the station.

'There are graves back there,' said Ayu, sounding surprised.

'Yes, there's a cemetery behind the station.'

'It'd be nice to be able to see the ocean forever.'

'It would,' I said, taking out my phone to message Mum.

Just arrived at the station. Can we go to the hospital?

Her reply came right away.

Your dad's got all sorts of tests he needs to do, and I've already started towards home. Could you two come to the house instead?

I told her we could and then slid my phone back in my bag. I was a little relieved. I wasn't quite ready, emotionally, so it was nice not to have to go straight to the hospital.

'Ayu, want to walk along the beach since we're here?'

'Yeah!'

We left the station and walked down the steps towards the gentle sound of the waves. There was no one on the beach, it being December, and there wasn't a single cloud in the bright blue sky, which seemed to merge with the ocean. The water glittered as it reflected the rays of sun.

Ayu pulled her hand from mine and raced off with cries of joy. I was about to warn her to be careful not to fall, but stopped myself. It was a soft, sandy beach. She wouldn't hurt herself even if she did fall, and I wanted to let her have fun in whatever way she wanted.

The chill wind of the ocean and the sparkling waves had a special energy you could only feel here.

Ayu came back, looking like she was enjoying herself, and innocently asked, 'Mum, did you play in this ocean when you were a kid?'

I nodded and looked out towards the horizon. 'I came here to play often.'

I'd come with my friends when I was in school. When I was little, I'd come with my brother and our dog, Rin. Whenever we brought her, Rin would play along the beach just as Ayu was doing now.

The ocean seemed unchanging, but it wasn't. The sky and shape of the clouds changed with the seasons, and the ocean would show a different side of itself. It was gentle in spring, fun in summer, contemplative in autumn and fierce in winter.

'You know, we used to play with sparklers here in the summer,' I said.

'You can light fireworks here?' She looked concerned. There were only a few places you were allowed to use fireworks in our neighbourhood.

I smiled when I saw her expression. 'I'm not sure about now, but it was fine when I was a kid so long as you cleaned up after yourself.'

I remembered those days as I spoke.

Yes, there we are, my brother and I, playing with fireworks. Rin sat a few paces behind us because she was afraid of them. We played with all sorts of handheld fireworks, but we always finished with sparklers. They were the ones Rin was least frightened of and liked the most, or at least liked enough to come to our side and look at them.

'That was so long ago . . .' I murmured.

'Mum, what's that island?' asked Ayu, pointing at an island jutting from the coastline.

'That's Enoshima Island.'

That place, too, held memories. I used to take Rin there for walks all the time. There were a lot of cats living on the island, and Rin was so gentle that she made friends with them. I wanted to take Ayu to Enoshima Island as well, but now wasn't the time for that.

'All right,' I said. 'We should head to Grandma's house.'

I held out my hand. Ayu nodded as she took it.

We climbed back up the stairs from the beach, the sound of the waves still audible behind us.

4

We continued down the residential streets with the ocean at our back and arrived at my childhood home. There was the plaque bearing the surname Hasegawa, my maiden name. The house had essentially no front garden, and there was just about enough space in the driveway to park a car. A white saloon always used to be parked there, but my parents didn't have a car anymore, ever since my father decided he was too old to drive. Instead, there were two bicycles and a few planters which Mum used for growing vegetables.

'Is this Grandma's house?' asked Ayu. I told her it was as I pressed the intercom.

No reply.

'I don't think Grandma's back from the hospital yet,' I said.

'We can't go in?'

'Don't worry. I have a key.'

After the big fight, I'd tried to return my key to my mother, but gave up when she insisted I keep it in case something happened to them. I unlocked the door and was struck with a familiar aroma when I stepped inside. It was a blend of the incense from the Buddhist altar – the sweet tea olive incense Dad always used – and Mum's cooking. It was the smell of home.

'It smells like Grandma,' said Ayu as she went in and opened the door to the right of the entrance hall. That door led into the family room, which led onto the dining room. The Japanese-style sitting room was behind the family room.

The family room had sofas and a table, with large windows and an enclosed veranda on the far side. Before my brother was born, it had been a normal veranda tacked onto the outside of the building, but it was draughty, so they'd renovated it to make it part of the house.

The veranda had a large pillar. I used to sit there, leaning my back against it as I read a book. Rin would join me and sit with her bum pushed right up against me. Whenever I said her name, she'd turn to look at me, panting happily. I found her so cute I'd pull her into a big hug, feeling her warmth and fur on my cheek. I loved her so very much.

By the time Rin was thirteen, she had difficulty moving. Her health regularly failed her, and the vet told us we should prepare for the worst, considering her age. I received the news of Rin's condition from Mum near the end of my first year at my first job out of uni. Actually, I now recall that also happened in December.

'The vet says she doesn't have long. Come home. Dad won't be home until late.'

I got the message in the early evening. I lied and told the people at work I wasn't feeling well before rushing out. But I was too late. Rin had stopped breathing by the time I arrived.

At first, I couldn't believe it. She lay on the veranda with her eyes closed. It looked as if she was sleeping there, as she usually did.

'Rin,' I called. Normally, she'd lift a sleepy head and smile at me, but she didn't this time.

I touched her. She was still warm, but her body was a little stiff. It didn't feel like the Rin I knew. That's when it finally hit me, that she was gone. I crouched beside her unmoving body and broke into sobs that wrenched themselves from somewhere deep in my throat.

I kept stroking her fur as I cried, 'I'm sorry, I'm sorry.' I'd brought her into our family, but I hadn't been there to see her out. I'd left home when I was needed most.

The memory made it hard to breathe, nearly bringing tears to my eyes.

After crying my eyes out, I apologised to Mum and left without staying the night. I said I'd be back the next day to lay Rin to rest. I did not want to see my father when I felt as if I was broken in both body and soul. I was certain he would have a go at me, saying Rin was my responsibility. I didn't think I could handle hearing it from him when I was already blaming myself.

I stood alone on the platform at Kamakura Kokomae Station under a pitch-black sky. The cold winter wind bit mercilessly at my tear-stained cheeks as I waited for the train. The pain from that day is still fresh, as if it happened only yesterday.

'Oh, Grandma,' I heard, bringing me back to reality. Ayu rushed to the front door, presumably having spotted her grandmother through the window.

'Ayu, no running in the house,' I called to her back as I wiped away the tears gathering in my eyes.

'Grandma!' she said.

'Oh, you made it. It's nice to see you, Ayu.'

Their happy voices made me smile.

'It's nice to see you, too, Junko,' my mother said when she came in. 'I'm sorry I'm so late. I stopped to do a bit of shopping on the way home.'

In each hand she carried a reusable shopping bag bursting with things, which she set on the table with a sigh.

'I could've done the shopping if you'd said something,' I said.

'But these are presents for Ayu.'

The bags were filled with snacks and toys. Ayu looked at them and her face brightened. 'Wow! It's *Shooting Star Angels*!'

'Everything in this bag is yours, Ayu, so go ahead and look through it,' said my mum as she pushed one of the bags towards my daughter.

'Thanks, Grandma!' Ayu carried the huge shopping bag over to the veranda and took out the items, one by one, with squeals of joy.

'Mum, you didn't have to,' I said. 'You're already dealing with so much right now.'

'It's the least I can do when my granddaughter comes to visit.'

'What happened to Dad?'

'He went to drink his morning cup of tea, but his

hands suddenly went numb and he dropped it. He couldn't really speak properly . . .'

'Oh gosh. What happened after that?'

'I was afraid it was something serious, so I called an ambulance right away. They said it was a good thing I reacted so quickly. They say he might not be as mobile after this, not as he used to be, but he'll live. The physiotherapy is going to be tough on him, I think, but I'm just glad he's alive.'

And she did truly seem to be.

'You've been through a lot, too, Mum,' I found myself murmuring.

She didn't seem to catch it and asked what I'd said, but I just shook my head and told her it was nothing.

'Right, well, let me show you what I've bought,' she said happily, getting ready to cook.

I smiled back. 'I'll help.'

We had sukiyaki for dinner. Ayu raved about how delicious it was, chattering happily with a smile on her face the entire time. 'We'll go and see Grandpa tomorrow, right?'

Mum seemed happy every time Ayu asked the question, but I felt conflicted.

When we had finished dinner, Mum took Ayu for a bath, after which Ayu fell asleep in the blink of an eye on the tatami-mat floor in the sitting room. She was probably worn out from travelling. I tutted, quickly laid out a futon and shifted her onto it. Mum was in the kitchen, watching me as she boiled the kettle. Her eyes were crinkled in a smile.

There was a Buddhist shrine in the Japanese-style sitting room. A photo of Rin sat there, likely put there by Mum. A tiny photo album also sat at the edge of the shrine. I picked it up gently to find it was filled with nothing but photos of Rin. My heart warmed at the images of her full of life. 'Oh, Mum . . .' I whispered.

'Junko, would you like a cup of tea?'

'Yes, please,' I called back, closing the photo album and setting it back in its place. I checked the blanket draped over Ayu one more time before going to the dining table.

'You know, Mum, you seem quite calm, all things considered. I thought you'd be a bit more frazzled, with Dad collapsing and all.'

'Oh?' Mum set two cups of tea at the table before lowering herself into a chair. 'Well, I was frazzled at first, when it happened. I expected the worst, but I was just so relieved when they told me he'd live.'

'Mm.' It seemed that domineering man was important to her.

'Besides,' she said, 'a life spent raising children gives you some steel.'

'I suppose you're right. I've only been a mum a short while, but I think I know what you mean.'

'I know it was so hard on you, trying to get pregnant, but I'm glad you never gave up.'

'Actually, I did,' I said with a pained expression. I was sitting across from her.

'What do you mean you did?'

'It was too hard to continue with the fertility treatment. I gave up.'

'Really . . .?'

It had been difficult, both mentally and financially.

'And I decided the part of me that thought I needed to have children had been created by the . . . curse Dad put on me.'

Mum blinked at me a few times, as if she didn't really understand what I meant.

'Dad always said women should marry early and have children, right?'

She seemed to get it then.

'And all of his emotional abuse remained as a sort of curse,' I explained. 'I felt like an idiot for being so desperate to have children when I realised that, so I gave up on the treatment. I gave up on it all.'

I had been utterly exhausted. When my husband

suggested we stop trying, having already put in so much effort, I felt a weight lift from my shoulders. I thought it could be just as incredible to spend the rest of our lives together, just the two of us. Giving up was a sort of acceptance. After that, seeing young children no longer put my heart in a tizzy. There remained a faint longing, the thought that it would be nice if the stars aligned and I became pregnant, but it wasn't the desperation from before. It wasn't an obsession.

'And then Ayu came along,' I said, leaning my cheek on my hand as I looked over at her sleeping.

I'd been dumbfounded when I became pregnant with her. I'd yearned for this miracle for so long, but I couldn't believe it when it finally arrived. Maybe it's always like that when your dream comes true.

'Oh,' whispered Mum, looking away. 'I'm sorry it turned into a curse for you.'

'You're not the one who needs to apologise. I know full well how you've struggled with him, too.'

She shook her head. 'It wasn't like that, Junko . . .'

My phone vibrated. It was a message from my husband, asking if now was a good time for a call. Mum seemed to notice and stepped away. 'I think I'll head to bed.'

'Goodnight,' I said.

I called my husband once Mum had left the family room.

'Hi. Sorry I haven't kept you updated. It looks like Dad is going to be all right,' I said.

'You'll be going to see him in hospital tomorrow?'

My husband was, of course, aware of my strained relationship with my father. I struggled to find the right words to answer his question, which arose from that awareness.

'Yeah,' I said finally. 'Ayu wants to meet her grandpa. To be honest, I don't want to go, but I also don't want to keep Ayu from her grandfather any longer for my own personal reasons.'

I could always stay at home while Mum took Ayu to see him, but I was afraid of what he might say to her.

'Right . . .' sighed my husband. I detected a note in his voice that told me he'd already guessed how I felt, mingled with a bit of relief. 'What's it like visiting Kamakura after all this time? I bet you can properly see the stars.'

I smiled. It was so kind of him to try to change the subject.

'The stars? Hm. I'm not sure they're really all that different from Tsukuba here.' Tsukuba was also the kind of place where you could see the stars twinkling in the night sky past midnight.

We chatted about this and that before I hung up and cleared the teacups from the table. When I went to the fridge for a drink of water before I took a bath, I realised there wasn't any milk. Ayu would want milk in the morning. I also wanted to make breakfast, as it was my first time back home in so long. Maybe French toast . . .

I might pop out to the convenience store.

I put on my coat and went outside. I made sure to lock the door before walking down the silent street. It was chilly, but not so cold it made you huddle into yourself. It was a pleasant coolness.

I looked up and saw a normal night sky. *I wonder what it would look like from the beach?* Wouldn't the beach be dangerous at this time of night? Well, I could go to the train station, at least. I was gripped by nostalgia as I walked along the night-time streets.

I craned my neck when the coast came into view and saw a faint light on the beach towards Enoshima Island. I squinted and just about managed to make out a truck of some sort.

What's that there for?

I went down the steps out onto the beach, listening to the waves as they washed in and pulled away. A half-moon hung in the night sky, below which sat a food truck café. In front of the food truck was a sign saying FULL MOON COFFEE SHOP and a single table.

Huh? I doubted my eyes. It was the same food truck that had been in Tsukuba Park. *They came all the way out here?*

A black cat sat atop the table, its long tail waving in time with the sound of the ocean. It turned to look at me and meowed.

5

I had a dream. A food truck café was on the beach, and a black cat talked to me. I looked back and saw me, as a child, along with my brother and our dog, Rin. We were playing with sparklers, which fizzled and sent embers scattering across the sand.

Why?

My heart filled with emotions, and I started to cry.

'Mum, are you okay?'

The voice woke me. Ayu was looking at me with concern while brilliant morning sunlight spilled through the veranda windows. I frowned.

Last night, I'd gone to the beach and seen a food truck

café. I didn't remember anything beyond that. I'd cried in my dream, and tears had spilled from my eyes in real life. The corners of my eyes and my temples were wet with tears.

'Mum, does your tummy hurt?' asked Ayu, her eyes narrowing as she looked at me with worry. She was so adorable that I pulled her into a tight hug.

'I'm fine. I just had a dream.'

'A sad dream?'

'I don't remember . . .'

I didn't really think it had been sad.

'All right,' I said, sitting up. 'I bet you're hungry. I thought I'd make breakfast this morning.'

The moment I spoke of food, my eyes snapped to the kitchen. There was a loaf of bread on the table, which I must have bought at the convenience store the night before. *So, I did go shopping . . .* I stood up and went to get the bread. I then went over to check the fridge and found milk.

'Mum, what's wrong?'

'Nothing,' I said, shaking my head. 'I'm going to make French toast.'

'Yay!' said Ayu, waving her hands in the air. The door to the living room opened and my mother came in and said good morning.

'Oh, you're making French toast?' she asked. 'That's sweet of you.'

'Morning, Grandma. We get to go and see Grandpa today, right?'

'That's right. Thank you for going. We'll take a taxi there.'

I watched their exchange and sighed over my warring emotions. But, unlike yesterday, I didn't feel an oppressive gloom.

Before we set off, Mum called the hospital to make sure it was all right for us to visit. My father was in the large general hospital in Fujisawa. We got out of the taxi and went into the lobby. Ayu's steps were light, even though she hated hospitals.

'Ayu, you normally dislike going to hospitals,' I said.

'It's not like I'm getting stuck with a needle today.'

Mum smiled at that.

My heart thudded with an unpleasant sound as we walked down the hall to his room. *How many years has it been since I've seen him?*

My chest tightened when I saw the name card on the door – Tatsuo Hasegawa. It looked as if he had a room to himself. Mum gave a short knock and then went in, without waiting for a response. 'We're here. How do you feel?'

'Ah . . . Much better.'

Hearing them talking, I froze in the hallway, unable

to move. Ayu, however, didn't hesitate in the slightest. She went straight into the room. 'Hello, Grandpa. Nice to meet you. My name's Ayu Ichihara,' she said, full of energy.

My eyes went wide, and I looked into the room. Dad was reclined in the bed, which was propped up to a forty-degree angle. In my mind, he'd always been a big man. He seemed to have become thinner and quite a bit smaller.

His eyes grew large when he saw Ayu.

'Look, Grandpa. This is Ayu. She's cute, isn't she?' said Mum, tears in her eyes as she happily stroked Ayu's hair. A smile crept onto his face, but his expression quickly clouded over when he noticed me standing by the door. He looked away.

'Mm,' he grunted, his only response to the proper greeting Ayu had given him.

That's right. That's the sort of person he is.

Anger bubbled up inside me, but none of it even seemed to register with Ayu. She moved over to the bed. 'Grandpa, thank you for the snacks and toys yesterday.'

'Huh?' His face screwed up.

'That bag was filled with so many of the things I like. It made me so happy!' Ayu continued.

In a fluster, Dad looked at Mum. 'Did you tell her?'

Mum shook her head. It was then that I finally realised she had only bought the toys and snacks for Ayu's visit because he had told her to. Ayu was more perceptive than the average person, meaning she realised right away the presents weren't filled just with her grandmother's love, but with her grandfather's too.

'I *love* that show *Shooting Star Angels*,' said Ayu. 'Do you know it, Grandpa?'

'Uh, no . . .'

'It's so cute. I like the Star girl.'

Ayu ploughed on, unfazed, with Dad making the occasional, uncomfortable comment. It was the kind of sight that brought a smile to people's faces. Seeing him like that threw me off.

'Ayu, sweetie, I'm going to go and grab a drink,' I said. I left the room, unable to stand it for a minute longer.

I headed for a corner where there were vending machines and some benches arranged to make a sort of rest area. I sat on an empty bench and let out a sigh.

Mum quickly appeared, probably concerned. 'Junko, are you okay?'

I looked into her eyes and realised then I was grimacing. 'What *was* that? That horrible, controlling man has grown old and is now socially awkward with his granddaughter?'

It was so sudden. I couldn't take it in, even though I'd seen it with my own eyes. I hung my head. Mum sat next to me.

'He's always been clumsy. That's all,' she said softly.

I couldn't reply, so Mum continued. 'And, when you think about it, when did he turn into such a bad man?'

'What do you mean?'

'Do you remember Maki? You were really attached to her.'

'Er, yeah. You mean the Maki who lived down the street?'

Maki was an older girl who lived in a house across the street. She was a university student and fluent in English, as well as being kind and intelligent. I admired her when I was little.

'That's right,' Mum said. 'She ended up getting a job overseas, and her mother was so sad. I told your dad I'd be proud of you if you dedicated yourself to your work one day and got a job overseas, but that I'd also be sad. He panicked after that. He wanted to keep you here, with us.'

I was lost for words. 'But he also did other things. He was always saying horrible things. Like when Rin came home . . .'

Dogs don't live long. She'll die soon, and you'll just be sad. I remembered his words and bit my lip.

'He was scared when he saw you so innocently happy with the dog, because he knew pets always die before their owners. He just wanted to prepare you for the truth, that dogs don't live as long as humans do and Rin would pass away before you.'

I felt lightheaded. I'd never even considered that possibility. 'What? But . . . Even so, he didn't have to go and say that. No matter how prepared you are for that eventuality, you'll still be sad when it happens.'

'I know,' she said with a weak smile. 'Your dad had a dog when he was a child, too, and he was very sad when it died. He couldn't help but say it. He's a very socially awkward person.'

I grimaced at how Mum kept using that phrase. 'But "socially awkward" doesn't explain it,' I said. 'He was too harsh on Jiro. He went too far.' I nodded to myself. What I had experienced was only a fraction. I couldn't help feeling bad over what my brother had gone through.

'But your father cared for Jiro in his own way, too,' said Mum. 'Jiro was such a fragile boy. Dad was hard on him so that he would be able handle the real world when he ventured out into it. And your grandfather . . . He was a very harsh person. Your dad thought that was the right way to be.'

I barely remembered my grandfather because he died when I was very young, but I had heard how harsh he was.

'Your father,' continued Mum, 'wanted to be a photographer when he was young, but his father didn't approve. He ended up getting a *real* job, and because he was fairly happy doing that, it convinced him that a parent is always right. So he tried to push that onto Jiro . . .'

'Wait, Dad wanted to be a photographer?' It was the first I had heard of it.

'He did. You know that photo album on the Buddhist shrine? Dad took all those photos of Rin using an SLR camera. He actually looked after her more than I did once you'd moved out.'

The pounding of my heart grew louder.

'It's true that a lot of what he did and said can't be explained away as mere awkwardness. He acknowledges that. That's why he accepted without arguing that you hate him. But he's still been trying to support you and Jiro from the sidelines.'

Some part of me had sensed it. Mum had helped me with so many things – university tuition fees, my wedding, after I'd had Ayu. I had suspected Dad was behind it a little. Not that I'd wanted to accept that . . .

My expression soured, and Mum let out a small sigh. 'He always insisted I not tell you, though.'

I looked at her with a question in my eyes.

'The day Rin died, and I told you Dad was working late . . . That was a lie.'

'You lied?'

'He told me to call and tell you he'd be away from the house when you came.'

My jaw dropped as my eyes widened.

'I know you've been through a lot of pain. But he's hurting too. That's all I want you to understand,' she said. With that, she stood up, told me she was going back to his room and left.

I watched her go in a daze. My mind was filled with confused static. My father was overbearing and emotionally abusive, the sort of person you'd call a toxic parent nowadays. He was not someone I could forgive.

And yet, to be told all those things . . .

As I was thinking, the sound of waves seemed to flood in from somewhere, bringing back vivid memories from the night before.

A half-moon floated above the night-time ocean. There was a food truck café called the Full Moon Coffee Shop on the beach. The black cat sitting on the table noticed me. It turned to me and said, 'Welcome. We've been waiting for you.'

I wasn't massively surprised to hear a cat speaking. It all felt like a dream. Besides, I was more surprised by what the cat had said. 'You've been waiting for me?'

'The master told you he would meet you again soon, didn't he?' said the cat, narrowing its violet eyes. It picked up the Reserved sign from the table and gestured for me to take a seat. It seemed the chair had been placed there just for me.

I sat down, thinking that everything about this seemed odd.

Then I suddenly looked up at the night sky to see the beautiful stars stretching out above me. I gasped. The winter constellations winked at me, but I didn't feel the chill I had felt earlier. The waves pulling in and out were like background music for the café.

As I drank in the starry sky, the master – the large tortoiseshell cat – came out. I remembered him. He stood in front of me and smiled.

'Let me welcome you again. The Full Moon Coffee Shop has no fixed location. It might appear in the middle of a familiar shopping arcade, by the station at the end of the railway line or on a quiet riverbank. At the Full Moon Coffee Shop, we don't take your order;

instead we bring you desserts, meals and drinks – selected just for you.'

I smiled back at him.

'I have prepared this drink for you,' he said placing a rather large glass in front of me. It was transparent and shaped like an ancient vase with no handles. Inside was tea, ice and a sparkler firing off bits of light. 'It is Sparkler Iced Tea.'

I brought my face close to the glass in astonishment, staring dubiously at the sparkler twinkling inside the liquid. *How in the world does it work?*

The master said, 'Tea and memories are extracted like leaping sparks. It will be ready to drink when the sparks have scattered and the last fragment falls.'

With that, he placed a straw in front of me and left.

'Tea and memories are extracted like leaping sparks . . .' I repeated, giggling and smiling at the poetic turn of phrase.

The amber sparks leaping in the dark tea were miraculously beautiful. I simply stared into the glass for a while, forgetting everything else, until I heard joyful cries from behind me. I turned around to see two children, a boy and a girl, playing with handheld fireworks – sparklers. A Shiba Inu stayed close by the girl's side.

I swallowed. It was us from a long time ago. Me, my brother, Rin . . .

We used to play with fireworks during the summers when I was in primary school. Behind the us of the past was a figure, an adult man. He stood there, saying nothing, watching over the children from a step away.

Dad.

Once we'd finished playing and were ready to go, Dad cleaned everything up without saying a word and led the way. I picked up Rin's leash and followed after him with my brother.

That's right. How could I have forgotten?

I only ever remembered the parts of my dad I hated. I'd blocked out all the wonderful memories of when we'd been close, like this one.

Clink came the sound of ice cubes shifting. The embers of the sparkler in the tea plopped down, and the vision of us as children faded like smoke.

Feeling as if I'd been under a spell, I picked up the straw and sipped the Sparkler Iced Tea. It was rich, but not bitter. And that faint sweetness . . . Was that honey? The flavour spread through my mouth, and I felt the heat of tears in the corners of my eyes.

'It's delicious,' I whispered.

'I'm glad,' I heard someone say.

I looked up and saw the black cat sitting in the chair across from me. I was surprised, but I leaned forward and asked, 'Was this table reserved for me?'

The black cat nodded. Its eyes, as beautiful as amethysts, were gleaming in the light.

'How did you know I'd be here? Did I make a reservation and forget about it?'

The black cat shook its head. 'You weren't the one who reserved it. Twenty-one years ago, we were asked to take care of you when you came.'

I started to ask who had made this request, but pressed my lips together instead. A figure appeared clearly in my mind. 'By Rin?' I asked.

The cat chuckled. 'Her name comes from the word for the cycle of reincarnation, doesn't it? It's a good name.'

Warmth bloomed in my chest. 'Thank you,' I said shyly. So, Rin had asked them to serve me before she left on her journey to the next world. The thought filled me with wonder.

'We're going to be bringing a dog into our family soon,' I said, 'and we've decided to name her Rin. The new Rin couldn't possibly be my old Rin reincarnated, right? That doesn't happen in waking life.' I chuckled at how I was almost talking to myself. I might as well have been, since everything I was experiencing was like a dream anyway.

The black cat's eyes narrowed slightly. 'Reincarnation is real. You know about the power you brought with you from your previous life, don't you?'

I remembered the blonde woman I had met at the fortune-telling corner in the shopping centre and nodded, though I was a little confused.

'People are reincarnated based on the good deeds of their previous life. However, those who have committed savage acts and cannot be considered human may be reborn as animals. And the opposite is also true.'

'Animals can be reborn as people?'

The black cat nodded. 'Animals that humans have loved dearly may be reborn as humans. But only if they want to be. That's why most animals who are reborn as humans were pets in their previous life.'

I looked at the cat, thinking about that possibility.

'Do you know why a pet might want to be reincarnated as a human?' asked the cat.

'Because they saw their human's life and were jealous?'

The cat chuckled. 'Most pets would never think that. Being human seems hard.'

I shrugged. That might be true.

'Despite the difficulty of human life, some pets want to be reborn as a human. They want it not for themselves, but to help the person they love. That's why many of them are special and born with skills normal people don't have. We call these precious beings "Children of the Stars".'

'Huh . . .'

Does that mean Rin was reincarnated as a person? I thought.

'She was.'

I looked up.

And there she was.

'Mum.' Ayu's voice brought me back to the present. I looked up and saw her poking her face into the rest area. She came straight towards me, and the black cat's words echoed in my mind: *Your family loved her so much. She was reborn and she wishes so very much to help you and your family.*

Fireworks seemed to spark inside me.

'Ayu!'

It was her! She had been reincarnated and come to save me. She saw me suffering from being unable to get pregnant, saw how our family was in pieces and she came to save us.

'Thank you, Ayu. Thank you for coming,' I said, squeezing her in my arms.

'Did you get lost, Mum?' She looked at me, taken aback.

I pressed my head against her tiny forehead. 'Yeah . . . I was lost.' *I truly was lost.* No, not even lost. I hadn't been able to move. I had been so weak. If I was upset with him, I should have confronted him properly. I needed to fight it out with him, to let our opinions collide. But I was afraid of him. So I cowered and ran.

'But I'm okay, now,' I said. 'Let's go.'

I took Ayu's hand and stood up.

'It's this way,' Ayu said. She genuinely seemed to believe I didn't know the way back to Dad's hospital room and took leading me seriously. My expression softened at the adorable sight, and I said to her back, 'You know, Ayu, I think I figured out what you were in your previous life.'

She turned back, her eyes shining. 'Really? What was I?'

'You were an angel.'

'Daddy always says I'm an angel too. Sato says you're both mushy parents.'

Ayu pouted at the answer, which wasn't what she'd been hoping for, and I chuckled.

We stepped into Dad's hospital room, and he looked at me with a sour expression. I would have been frightened before, but not anymore. I felt as calm as the smooth sea. I'd always thought I wanted him to apologise to me if I ever saw him again. But, oddly, now that I was facing him, a part of me wondered if I should be the one to apologise. Though I suppose we'd both hurt each other and gone beyond the point of simply saying sorry.

'It was a shock to hear you'd collapsed, but I'm glad it didn't turn out to be more serious,' I said. Dad's eyes went wide.

His mouth opened to say something, and then closed again. I could see his face turning redder by the second, which I guessed could have been him holding back tears. He turned away and grumbled, 'You say that, but I won't be able to move my legs without physiotherapy. It's a right pain.'

Ayu leaned towards him and said, 'Then you'll have to work hard at physiotherapy.' He froze, and Ayu went on. 'Because I want to go and play with sparklers on the beach in the summer.'

Dad trembled slightly before letting out a sound of acknowledgement that was so faint I barely caught it.

'Oh, dear,' Mum said, bringing her hand to her mouth. 'Well, you can't argue with your granddaughter, can you? I suppose you'll just have to give the physiotherapy your all.'

He looked away with a sullen expression. I hadn't managed to understand him in the past when he was like this. I'd wonder why he was so unfriendly all the time, making me scared and uncomfortable. Now I realised he was just embarrassed. At some point, I'd grown into an adult able to see her parents objectively.

'Oh, that's right . . .' started Mum, but there came a knock on the open door.

Everyone looked up. Standing in the doorway was a man in his early forties. He was slender, with a three-day beard. His hair, curled and longish, was pulled back in a messy little ponytail that came down to the nape of his neck. He wore a jacket and jeans in a rough, casual style that still managed to be fashionable.

'Jiro . . .'

It was my little brother. He bobbed a bow in greeting and stepped into the room. 'You seem to be doing all right, Dad.'

Dad grunted in acknowledgement, looking thrown entirely off balance.

'Can't say I haven't got all sorts of thoughts about this situation, but, well, I couldn't help worrying when I heard what happened,' said Jiro with a teasing smile.

Jiro had started using an *onē* form of speech after that altercation, and that hadn't changed.

Ayu looked at me and whispered, 'Who's that?'

Jiro had avoided Ayu, saying he wasn't sure it was right for her to meet someone like him.

'He's my brother,' I said. 'Your Uncle Jiro.'

'Ouch,' said Jiro, with his hands on his cheeks. 'That stings, being called "Uncle".'

But Ayu didn't mind his reaction. She walked up to Jiro and chirped, 'It's nice to meet you. My name is Ayu Ichihara.'

'Oh, no, sweetie. We've met before, when you were just a little baby.' He pinched her cheek.

'But I don't remember that.'

'I wouldn't think so. Anyway, call me Jiro-chan. Don't call me uncle, okay?' He laughed and stroked her hair.

Dad cleared his throat quietly and, with his eyes still averted, said, 'Jiro.'

Jiro turned towards him. 'Yeah?'

'I heard you got married.'

The news of Dad's collapse had completely eclipsed the news of Jiro's marriage in my mind, but I had been surprised by it at the time. I hadn't been certain if our parents knew, but it sounded as if Jiro had told them before Dad collapsed and even before he had told me. I assumed he was married to a man, which was another can of worms. I imagined that hearing of his marriage would have been far more of a shock to my parents than it was to me. In fact, part of me suspected that the news might have actually been what caused Dad's collapse.

Jiro nodded and said yes, he was married.

'I see,' Dad grumbled. Then he opened his mouth again to say, 'I was worried you'd spend your entire life alone. I feel a bit better knowing you've found someone to share your life with.'

His words shocked me. And they seemed to shock Jiro, too. He froze, his eyes wide.

'Oh my, you really surprise me, Dad. I didn't expect you to say something like that.' Jiro laughed, perhaps trying to hide the tears pooling in his eyes, before wrapping his arms around himself. 'And, actually, my partner's here, if you'd like to . . .'

Jiro turned to the door, and our eyes met unexpectedly. 'Jiro,' I said. 'I'm not sure that's a good idea. Too much shock at once . . .'

Talking about his partner and actually meeting them were two very different things. Wouldn't it be wiser for them to wait until Dad was a little more used to the idea?

But, despite my panic, Dad smiled slightly. 'Well, it's a long trip to make for nothing. Come on in.'

It seemed no one had changed more than our father while our family had been broken apart. He'd become estranged from his children and retired from the job he'd worked at for so many years. And perhaps that had given him more time for introspection than us.

Jiro smiled and thanked him before turning to the door and calling, 'Sorry for the wait. Come on in.'

And then a woman in her late twenties entered the room. She was wearing a navy suit and carrying the sort of fruit basket you bring sick people. She looked intelligent, and I had the feeling I'd seen her somewhere before.

Ayu cried out, 'It's the person who made *Shooting Star Angels*!'

Jiro nodded. 'This is Akari Nakayama. She's a TV producer. And little Ayu's right: she's in charge of *Shooting Star Angels*.'

Akari seemed rather nervous. Her expression was tense as she said, 'I-it's nice to meet you,' and gave an awkward little bow.

We bowed back, all dumbfounded. Dad's mouth hung open, and Mum said, 'Oh dear,' as she pressed her hand to her cheek. 'We assumed Jiro would have married a man, being an *onē* . . .'

Both Dad and I looked at her in shock for saying exactly what she was thinking without filter.

Jiro laughed. 'To be honest, I have dated men.'

This time Akari looked at Jiro with surprise. 'But you told me you're attracted to women.'

'I am. It's just, at the time, I didn't really know who I was. I was wandering around, lost. But once you turn forty, it stops being about men or women, you know? It did for me, anyway. But Akari, you're smart, and good at your job, and gorgeous. You're a top-class lady, flawless in every way. And if we're being honest, someone like me is sort of taboo for someone like you, but you said you love me for who I am, all of me. That's something you want to protect for your whole life, isn't it?'

Mum and I brought our hands to our mouths and said, 'Aw.' Akari turned bright red and looked down at the floor. Dad's mouth turned up slightly at the corners. He looked to Akari and said, 'Akari, please take good care of him.'

She met his gaze firmly and said, 'I will. Thank you for letting me join the family.' Then she gave a deep bow.

Warmth spread through my chest, and Ayu gently squeezed my hand. I looked down at her. She was grinning, looking back up at me. 'This is nice, isn't it, Mum?'

I was so moved tears spilled down my face. I nodded and stroked Ayu's hair.

Ayu ran straight over to Akari and told her how much she loved *Shooting Star Angels*. Then she proceeded to tell everyone we were adopting a dog – including the fact that we were naming her Rin.

Jiro crossed his arms and said, 'Huh,' in surprise.

Our scattered family was now in one space, laughing

together. It was only now, being there, that I realised exactly how much I'd hoped to see this someday. At the centre was Ayu, chatting happily, which brought back memories of Rin from long ago.

Thank you, I whispered to myself.

Epilogue

流星群のポップコーン

While the stars have shone unchanging in the sky for the past several millennia, people's lives on Earth have been woven through with all sorts of emotions. There is joy and sorrow, misunderstandings and disagreements.

And the servants of the stars labour to help them, if only just a little.

After working tirelessly, they gathered on the night of Christmas Eve in the rooftop garden of the Asakura Museum of Sculpture for their end-of-the-year party.

*

'I bet Junko and her family are having a lovely Christmas Eve,' I murmured while bringing some Meteor Shower Popcorn to my mouth. I couldn't get enough of the sweet caramel sauce perfectly balanced out with salt. It was the one essential at our parties.

I closed my eyes and watched the people I'd met flicker across the back of my eyelids. Their new family member, Rin, had just joined them in their home. Junko's father had lost some of his mobility after collapsing, but he was soon discharged from the hospital and could now see his granddaughter while he kept up with his physiotherapy. It looked as if they were all having a Christmas Eve party together.

Satomi seemed to be having a wonderful time with her boyfriend. And Koyuki must have taken that Christmas cake home to her family. She looked renewed. She'd opened a new door in her life, and I was certain it would lead to all sorts of incredible things.

'That's right,' I murmured, opening my eyes. 'Koyuki has a Pisces Moon sign, and so does Junko.'

Luna, who was sitting next to me, nodded and said, 'They do, Venus.'

We'd only just been talking about how Moon signs aren't as capable of bringing their power to the fore as Sun signs are.

'But,' said Luna, 'the immature Moon sign often holds hints to what our true wishes are.'

I cocked my head, not entirely sure I understood what she'd said.

She chuckled and smiled. 'At its heart, Pisces is a sign of tolerance, healing and forgiveness.'

'That's right,' I said. 'Many Pisces Sun people are very open-minded. And not just towards others, but towards themselves . . .' I understood that much, but then my eyes went wide. 'But both Koyuki and Junko, who have Pisces Moon signs, had a strong desire to forgive but found it hard to actually do so.'

Both of their true wishes were to forgive, and they were in pain because they couldn't do so properly.

Luna nodded. 'It's not uncommon for people with the Pisces Moon sign to want to forgive more than others, but they complicate things because they struggle to do so.'

'So what should they do in that situation?'

'The first step is to forgive yourself. Forgive yourself for resenting others, being jealous of others, being unable to forgive others. The world's laws are all a mirror, and everything begins with yourself. If you forgive yourself, you'll be able to forgive others. But many people don't realise that. They continue the cycle as if nothing's wrong, and that's not limited to people with Pisces as their Moon signs.'

Luna gave herself a deprecating smile before saying, 'It's ironic, isn't it?'

But I smiled warmly. 'In spite of it all, the two of them managed to forgive themselves.'

'They did. And that's something to be celebrated.'

'It really is.' I looked up into the night sky.

The Full Moon Coffee Shop was usually only open on nights with a full or new moon. Tonight, though, we had special hours for Christmas Eve, meaning the moon was lacking. It felt a bit odd seeing the moon like this, having always seen it as a perfectly round disc.

Perhaps when Luna talked about the moon being immature, she was referring to how it was unstable and changed shape. That, and how the moon only shines under the sun's light.

'Oh,' I whispered, as I stared up at the moon.

'What?' asked Luna.

'I get it now. The secret of Moon signs.'

'Hm?' Luna frowned.

'Because they're immature and unstable, they only shine when we cast light on them.'

'What?'

'Like, someone with a Pisces Moon sign can't hold a candle to someone with a Pisces Sun sign, which is why they often develop an inferiority complex about it. But that's why, that's exactly why, we shine a light on them, because that's how they realise their true wish.'

Luna's eyes grew wide.

To shine a light on someone.

The exact method will vary from person to person, whether it's forgiving yourself or accepting something. The Moon might not be able to look directly at the Sun's brilliant light, but it still admires the Sun deep in its heart, and it's just that – being illuminated by the Sun's light – that allows the Moon to shine.

'Perhaps,' Luna said, looking away to hide the tears pooling in her eyes.

Jupiter stepped between us. 'What a lovely night. Let's make another toast.' She raised her glass, her arms draped around our shoulders.

As she did, Saturn gave an exasperated sigh. 'You really like toasts, don't you?'

'I just think it's a blessing to be able to say "Cheers!" with everyone while filled with joy.'

Luna chimed in with quiet agreement before looking at Saturn. 'I get the impression you'd rather give a eulogy than a toast.'

'Even you, our calm and collected Luna, see me that way . . .'

Luna giggled and apologised. It made me happy to see her smile; her expression was normally so blank.

'Yes, let's do another toast,' I said. 'Wait, but first, Jupiter, tell us what Luna's cocktail means – her Violet Fizz.'

'Why not?' said Jupiter with a teasing smile. She laid a finger along Luna's glass and said, 'The meaning of this beautiful violet cocktail is "remember me".'

Luna's eyes crinkled in a smile at that moment. 'It suits me perfectly. I'm always thinking that.'

'Really?' I asked.

'Yep. That's why I project such strong energy on nights of the new moon, when you can't see me.'

Luna then raised her glass, said, 'Cheers!' and drank.

'Wait, Luna! We're supposed to do it together,' said Jupiter.

'Oh, it's fine,' I said with a smile. I copied Luna and drank my Wine Cooler.

'Luna, you do seem to do things your own way,' said Saturn with a sigh.

'Sorry,' said Luna. She didn't sound it.

I smiled at the two of them.

In the night sky was the gentle curve of the moon and the clear form of the Milky Way, with the twinkling stars swimming like fish through the river of the heavens.

Afterword

Thank you for reading *Best Wishes from the Full Moon Coffee Shop*. This is Mai Mochizuki.

This book is set at the end of 2020, and, while there is a faint hint of it, I didn't fully touch on the coronavirus. This is primarily because I wanted to be able to forget about masks and social distancing – in stories, at least. I appreciate your understanding of that decision.

While this book is the second in a series, I think it would be fine to start with it, though I also believe that if you read *The Full Moon Coffee Shop* first you will find this book easier to understand and more enjoyable. So, please, if you would like to, do so.

When I was writing the first book, I set out to create something that my readers could understand without having to read up on Western astrology. I was happy to hear from readers who already had some interest in astrology that the book was easy to understand, and that it even inspired them to take a look at their own natal chart. However, some people who had never dealt with astrology before said they had a hard time wrapping their heads around it and found the astrology parts of the book difficult. With that feedback in mind, in this book I decided to focus the astrology on Sun signs, Moon signs and Ascendants, because I think one of the first steps people can take is to look at their natal chart and check those three things, so they can confirm certain aspects of themselves.

One point I really would like to stress is that when it comes to astrology, there are as many interpretations as there are astrologers. This book was written using my interpretations as guided by the astrologer Eriko Miyazaki. It is possible that what I wrote here differs from how you see things, and in those moments, I ask that you not think in terms of who is and isn't correct, but rather that this is the interpretation in this story.

In the afterword of the first book, I briefly touched on what led to me taking up the study of astrology. Before writing this one, I thought back and realised that my original feelings of simply wanting to learn it really stemmed from a desire to increase my good fortune. Essentially, I wanted to make my own wish come true.

That's why I took a good look at my own wishes as

I studied astrology. When I did that, I was surprised to find that I really didn't know what my true wish was.

But, I thought, *do people really need to go out of their way just to know what it is they truly wish for? Doesn't everyone already know something like that?*

That's something Venus said in the book, and honestly, I thought that too in the beginning. I thought it was a given that I would know what I truly wished for. But I didn't. I was slightly off the mark with my true wish.

What I wanted at the time were things like winning the lottery, succeeding at my diet or becoming a published author. I discuss in this book how wishing to win the lottery is not really a true wish, so I won't touch on that here. Wanting to succeed at my diet came from thinking that if I was thin, I would be beautiful, but that meant my wish should have been 'to be beautiful', not 'to diet successfully'. My initial wish was just a little off from my true wish.

As regards becoming a published author, I just wanted to get something in print, because at the time I'd released several things I'd written on the internet. When I really asked myself which of my works I'd like to see published, there was one I thought had powerful emotions, but it was quite long, and another that I thought would be too difficult for readers. Still, I'd put so much effort into them that I wanted something to come of them, even though I didn't have a concrete plan on how to make that happen. And that's no good.

So, first things first, I decided that I needed to sort out what I really wanted. Once I'd worked through that, I realised that my wish was to publish a book through a traditional publisher, though I hadn't decided specifically which book. With that in mind, I looked again at the stories I had written and decided that, while they were all powerful, I couldn't see any of them becoming published books. And if that was the case, I decided, I should simply write a new book that *could* get published. That book ended up winning an award and leading us here.

That is how knowing your true wish can open your fortunes to you. But before you reach your true wish, you must sort through and know your own heart. I believe our Sun sign, Moon sign and Ascendant can give us hints towards that. The Moon sign in particular is said to represent our most basic self, our instincts even, and there are some things you can learn about yourself – just as the characters in this book do – if you examine it. There are, by the way, many different interpretations of the Moon signs within the field of astrology. I wrote this book while taking a close look at the Moon signs as well as my own personal feelings.

Right, now on to a little peek at the story of this book. To be honest, when the publisher first approached me to talk about a potential second book, I had almost no ideas for one. I was, of course, overjoyed at the prospect, but panicked when I couldn't think of anything to write about. After all, the first book wrapped up so nicely, wouldn't it be hard to write a sequel? It would be better not to write anything at all than something that was less than my best, wouldn't it? Shouldn't I just apologise and refuse the offer?

Just as I was agonising over what to do, Chihiro Sakurada posted her latest Full Moon Coffee Shop illustration on social media. It was called *Sparkler Iced Tea*. I was dumbstruck. It was beautiful and dreamy, and somehow nostalgic.

A video played in my mind as I looked at this incredible illustration. The scene with the Sparkler Iced Tea in Chapter 3 is exactly what I saw at that time, unchanged.

I also came up with a plot for the second book – a rough one, at least. It's odd to create a plot based on advice you received in a dream, but the culmination of that is this book. Now that the second book is finished, it warms my heart to know I've written something good that, while still me, has a different tone from the first book. From the bottom of my heart, I am grateful the stars brought me together with everyone who helped with this – in particular, Chihiro Sakurada for her incredible illustrations and Eriko Miyazaki for her continued guidance.

Thank you so very much.

I hope all your wishes come true.

Mai Mochizuki

This brazen book was created by

Publisher: Romilly Morgan
Junior Commissioning Editor: Jane Link
Editorial Assistant: Emily Campbell
Translator: Jordan Taylor
Senior Editor: Alex Stetter
Copy Editor: Caroline Taggart
Creative Director: Mel Four
Typesetter: Six Red Marbles UK
Production Controller: Sarah Parry
Sales: Lucy Helliwell, Rachael Lowth, Sammy Luton, Sophie Ramage
Publicity & Marketing: Chloë Johnson-Hill, Matthew Grindon, Charlotte Sanders

About the Author

Mai Mochizuki is the author of *The Full Moon Coffee Shop* and winner of the Everystar Ebook Grand Prix. She is a member of Mystery Writers of Japan and Unconventional Mystery Writers Club.